DANCER OF THE NILE

Veronica Scott

DEDICATION

To my daughters Valerie and Elizabeth

Acknowledgement

The Formatting Fairies!

CHAPTER ONE

The chariot jounced over deep, hard ruts, and Nima had to grip the railing tight with her bound hands to avoid falling. As the ride smoothed out again, she tossed her head to keep stray tendrils of hair out of her eyes and squinted, glancing behind at her fellow Egyptian prisoner. About an hour ago, a small unit had joined the bigger column that held Nima, dragging this man with them. The Hyksos had stripped him of his uniform and weapons, leaving him clad only in his loincloth and sandals as they forced him to march behind the chariot.

He was in a much worse state than she, beaten, staggering, arms bound cruelly tight behind his back. A black eye, cuts and spectacular bruises marred his tall, muscular frame, but he held his head high, cursing their captors as they prodded him to walk faster. The jaunty young officer strutted with pride as he discussed his successful capture of this soldier with the senior officer in charge of the entire column.

Taking note of the strength the Egyptian soldier showed as he strode along, she counted his old injuries and scars. *A handsome face, under the bruises. How had they managed to capture such a seasoned warrior?*

Nima flexed her hands, trying to ease the irritation from the ropes restraining her wrists. Angry red welts burned and itched where the hemp had chafed over the five long days of her captivity. *At least I'm allowed to ride in the captain's chariot, not trudging along in the dust and heat like the new prisoner.* Raising her head, she contemplated the blazing sun. *I'd have died the first day.*

The column halted, the soldiers and horses resting and sharing water. Her portion was brought to her in a small mug as she sat on the edge of the chariot. The soldier who handed her the water took his chance to fondle her breast for a moment through the thin, dusty, blue fabric of her dress before striding away with a laugh.

"Son of a jackal," she cursed as he cast another leering glance over his shoulder. Nima lifted the cup to her lips awkwardly then stopped, gazing over the edge of the unglazed mug to where the other prisoner knelt in the sand, head down, shoulders slumped. *They don't offer him water?*

How far can I push my status as Amarkash's personal prisoner? Inwardly quaking, Nima stood and took a few tentative steps in the direction of her fellow countryman. Most of the enemy soldiers were ignoring her in their own efforts to relax or drink water. The few who were facing in her direction didn't seem to care what she did, and the captain was at the end of the column, conferring with the younger officer stationed there. Hurrying the last few paces to the prisoner, Nima tried not to spill any precious water.

"Here," she whispered, holding the mug out to him. "Drink quickly."

When he raised his head, she recoiled from the intensity in his eyes, an unusual hazel with glints of green. *However defeated he may appear, this man isn't giving up.* Unsmiling, the warrior glanced at her bound wrists then at her face, saying nothing.

Why doesn't he trust me? Can't he see I'm a prisoner here, too? Nima placed the mug against his swollen, split lips and tipped it up. Swallowing in greedy gulps, he kept his eyes on her face.

She took the mug before he had drained all the water and drank the last few drops herself. A change in his expression gave her a split second of warning before Captain Amarkash grabbed her by the shoulder, yanking the cup from her hand and hurling it away. He slapped her face, cursing at her in his native tongue. Trying to soothe the sting, Nima put her hand to her cheek as Amarkash dragged her toward the chariot. Dimly, she was aware of the captive warrior struggling to his feet in an instinctive attempt to help her. She heard the soldiers beating him as she was hustled to the chariot and thrown into the vehicle.

"You do nothing without my permission, you understand?" Amarkash gave her another rough shake as he got into the chariot next to her. Shaking his finger under her nose, he said, "Stay away from the other prisoner."

Nima nodded. Amarkash had made it clear he was the only barrier standing between her and the soldiers, so the need to keep him placated outweighed sympathy for her countryman. "I understand. I thought he should have water--"

"This is not your concern. If I wish him to have water, *I'll* order it." Amarkash's command of Egyptian was amazingly good, his accent nearly flawless. Nima was constantly surprised how fluent he was. She'd learned a few words and phrases of Hyksos in the last five days, but he habitually spoke to her in her own language. He glared at her for another long minute, hand half raised as if to strike her again, but then he turned to snap the reins, and gave the column the order to proceed.

Clutching the chariot rail tightly, she risked one more glance over her shoulder. The prisoner was on his feet, marching along, fresh cuts on his face bleeding sluggishly where he'd been struck after trying to help her.

His presence complicates everything. Nima narrowed her eyes, glaring at the soldier.

Marching in the middle of the column, flanked by foot soldiers, Kamin watched the other prisoner out of the corner of his eye. At first he'd assumed she was with the Hyksos willingly, until he saw the ropes on her wrists. Yet they gave her quite a bit of latitude, even letting her share her water with him. At least until the officer intervened, plainly not wanting the two captives to interact.

She's brave. And kind. Battered and bruised Kamin might be, but he wasn't in the Afterlife yet. He'd noticed how attractive she was, even in her current condition. Slender, graceful. *A beautiful face, under the dust and fading bruises.* Staring at her took his mind off his aching muscles and precarious situation.

Set's teeth, but her presence complicates things. If the Hyksos gave him the slightest chance, he knew he could escape. He'd lay odds they weren't used to dealing with one of Pharaoh's Own Regiment. Let them think him a poor, terrified soldier, lower their guard. But now he had to consider the girl's welfare, too — no Egyptian woman could be abandoned to the depraved cruelties of the Hyksos. Her presence meant any plot to escape must now also be a rescue mission.

Sweat trickled down his spine. *Will she be able to help me work out some scheme for our escape? Will she be willing to try?* She wasn't particularly afraid of their captors, as far as he could see. Depending on how many more days of travel they had before reaching the main Hyksos' encampment, maybe he'd have another chance to communicate with her.

The ropes bit into his arms and shoulders, which had gone numb hours ago. Kamin tried to flex his muscles a little, to get some relief, but the knots were too tight. Trudging along like this was awkward, but he could keep going as long as the Hyksos could. *Longer!* Remembering how sweet the water had been, he licked his dry lips. *Better think about something else, anything else.* He observed the territory they were passing through, creating a mental map, so he could return to his own lines once he'd escaped. *I will escape, gods willing.*

Despite his determination, Kamin was nearly exhausted by the time the column halted for the day. The Hyksos had taken another water break, but the girl made no effort to come near him. A jeering guard had poured a few drops of water over Kamin's head, enough to torture his thirst but not quench it.

As the chariots were drawn into a circle and the soldiers made camp, Kamin was led off to the side. Laughing, a guard kicked his legs out from under him, so he collapsed to the sand. The Hyksos bound his legs before freeing his arms, which were completely numb and useless. Biting his lips till he drew blood against hot needles of pain, Kamin waited out the agony of feeling returning to his arms. His captors redid the bonds so he could feed himself with difficulty but not escape, yoking him by the neck to a chariot wheel before walking away.

Watching the activity in the camp, he assessed the odds against him. A tent was assembled for the captain, who promptly disappeared inside, leaving the junior officer in charge. The girl was taken to the cooking fire and her hands untied. Using supplies and fresh game the Hyksos brought over, she prepared a hot meal. The rich meaty aroma of whatever she was cooking made Kamin's stomach rumble, but he kept his face impassive, not wanting to give his captors any satisfaction, no hint he was suffering in any way, not even from hunger.

First the girl took portions to the two officers, then the soldiers formed a line, and she spooned stew into bowls as the men walked by, helping themselves to bread in a basket and passing wineskins through the ranks. Kamin heard snatches of ribald remarks, which she studiously ignored.

Following the flurry of activity, she finally took notice of him, resting her hands in her lap. Rising after a moment, she strolled into the tent.

Well, no food for me tonight. I'm not begging them to feed me. Kamin locked his hunger away with his other aches and pains. The churning acid in his gut couldn't interfere with his attempts to plan for any chance to escape. He'd gone without food before.

The tent flap fluttered a moment or two later, drawing his attention. *The girl.* Feeling hollow, stomach growling at him like a starving beast, he watched her movements.

Walking straight to the kettle, she ladled out a generous bowl full of stew, grabbed a chunk of bread and crossed the camp to him.

Kamin straightened against his restraints as she approached.

"Captain Amarkash said you could eat but not drink," she whispered when she got close, holding out the bowl and the bread. A dubious frown crossed her face as she focused on the ropes binding his wrists. "Can you manage?"

He extended his bound arms, hands cupped to take the steaming bowl. "Thank you, my lady. The gods bless you."

"If they truly blessed me, I wouldn't be here." She stuck the bread in the stew and placed the meal in his waiting hands. "Eat fast. He's just as likely to change his mind."

No sooner had she offered this advice than a harsh yell erupted from across the camp. "Nima!"

Closing her eyes, she turned. The Hyksos captain scowled at them, standing in front of his tent, hands on hips, eyes narrowed. He beckoned to her, and without another glance at Kamin she walked away.

At least I know her name now. Kamin kept his eyes on the interaction between her and the captain outside the tent as he awkwardly wolfed the dinner she'd provided. *I hope she isn't going to get in trouble for giving me food.* With each bite of the savory, lightly spiced, meaty stew, strength flowed to his muscles.

Nima was resisting some request or command from the officer. Finally the man pulled a long knife. Kamin tensed, testing the strength of the ropes, although there was nothing he could do to defend her. *Am I to watch her die because of kindness to me? But she said he'd given permission.*

After slitting the ropes on the woman's wrists, the captain seized her dress, yanked the already ragged garment over her head and threw it on the ground at her feet. She stood there calmly, her body now concealed only by a semi-sheer linen breast band and knee-length shift. He reached out to tug at the torn blue ribbon holding her long, messy braid, releasing her silky black hair to cascade onto her shoulders. The soldiers whistled, making crude comments in Hyksos. Setting the bowl carefully off to the side, Kamin stared, surprised to see the men settling in a big circle next to the fire..

Head high, Nima walked into the center of the circle, lifting her arms to the sky in a graceful arc. She nodded, and a soldier with a small flute launched into a discordant tune while the man next to him pounded a steady drumbeat on an overturned kettle. On tiptoe, Nima pirouetted into the first steps of a dance.

Kamin watched in disbelief at first. *Is she a kidnapped priestess, doing some sacred dance?* Clearly, she was well trained, her movements rhythmic despite the wretched music. As the dance progressed, he sensed she was cutting some movements short, editing others out completely, trying not to arouse her volatile audience too much. *I don't know about them, but she's certainly having an effect on me. This woman is as good as the best dancers in Thebes.* A vision of how her slender body would appear, bare-breasted, clad only in the short fringed skirt of a Theban dancer, flashed in his mind's eye.

Angrily, he shook his head, the rope cutting into his neck. *I should be trying to escape while they're all distracted, not mooning over some dancer like a cadet.* Surreptitiously, he reached out to catch the lip of the bowl, drawing it closer. He smashed it on a rock next to him, keeping the biggest jagged fragment and hastily sweeping sand over the others. Moving slowly, so as not to draw attention, he sawed at the tether holding him by the neck to the chariot wheel.

Finishing with a series of acrobatic moves, Nima practically landed in the lap of the junior officer. He shoved her to her feet, goggling anxiously at Amarkash, who was stalking toward them, snatching her dress from the ground as he came. She moved to meet the captain, accepting her garment and shrugging awkwardly into the garment.

Sorry the dance had ended, although puzzled at the awkward finale she'd done after the skill of the performance, Kamin narrowed his eyes, leaning against the wheel to ease the strain on the rope at his neck. The woven hemp was proving frustratingly impervious to his jagged shard. *Is she trying to conceal something?*

No sooner had the thought crossed his mind than Amarkash was yanking at her arm, the younger officer shouting and the soldiers scattering as she brandished a knife she'd evidently stolen from the man she had jostled.

Nearly breaking her slender wrist, Amarkash wrenched the blade free. He flipped the knife to the other officer with a curse, then dragged Nima into the tent, closing the panel behind them. A single scream from the tent, followed by silence, left Kamin cursing, bile rising in his throat.

Next morning, the girl was sullen, fresh bruises on her face when she walked out of the tent behind Amarkash and was assisted into the chariot by a soldier. Wrists tightly bound behind her, she stayed in the chariot or next to it during the hours of marching and the few stops made for resting the horses and men. Nima never glanced at Kamin. After a quick assessment at the start of the day to reassure himself she was more or less unharmed, Kamin deliberately averted his gaze. Something about her, not only the undeniable beauty, but also her bravery in this situation, touched him. Her attitude made him all the more determined to rescue her as well as extricating himself from the current predicament.

If only they didn't guard me so closely on the march. He glanced at the four soldiers marching in formation around him, spears and knives ready to take him down if he made any move to escape. His planning centered around a break after dark. *They're much less alert once they've made camp and had dinner.*

During the rest breaks, Amarkash personally gave Nima water to drink and allowed no opportunity for her to share. Soldiers provided Kamin with small sips of water every other rest stop, with much jeering and insults. He didn't care. Let them enjoy themselves as long as they gave him the precious water. Maintaining his strength was essential in this heat, not his dignity.

The column stopped before sunset, camping in a small oasis.

Curious about what would happen this evening, his attention was drawn to Nima, in tense discussion with the Hyksos captain. As he watched, the ropes on her arms were slashed, and she was given a small basket. Escorted by a soldier, she harvested plants of some sort from the overgrown gardens left by the former residents of the tiny oasis.

Going to the fire where her big stewpot glowed red hot, Nima busied herself with serious cooking. Pleased by her grace, her beauty, her stubborn refusal to give in to the terror of her situation, Kamin found some relief from his own aches and pains in observing her activities.

Him, they could only torture and kill. They could inflict much worse on her. Plainly, the Hyksos soldiers harbored some lingering hope of being allowed to assault her, touching her lasciviously whenever the captain's attention was elsewhere. *But the captain has staked his claim, and they all fear him enough to restrain themselves until he tires of her, which I suppose is a mercy.* Nima slapped one man's hands away with a curse. *She's strong.* Kamin looked again. *Or in shock.*

Tonight's meal smelled even better than the stew the night before. Sundown breezes brought a whiff his way, causing painful cramps in his gut, which grumbled.

Finally, after the officers and the soldiers had been fed, she scooped a bowl full of stew from the kettle and sauntered in his direction, her walk unhurried. Kamin enjoyed the view, realizing with a little jolt of dismay how eagerly he was anticipating even the most fleeting contact with her.

She set the bowl in his outstretched palms and looked him straight in the eyes, her own gaze intense. "Don't eat it," she said in a barely audible whisper, before walking away without a backward glance.

The guards watched him so he made a show of fumbling with the bowl, as if trying to get a better grip. He allowed the bowl to slip from his fingers, struggling against the ropes in a convincing show of desperation, attempting to catch it as it rolled off his fingertips. The bowl shattered on a rock, splattering him with stew. The guards standing nearby howled at his predicament. Kamin glared at them before bringing his greasy fingers to his lips, as if to lick some nourishment at least. Tempting as the aroma was, he didn't actually touch his tongue to the drippings.

I hope she knows what she's doing.

Kamin set himself to the task of blocking out the pain from his wounds, his hunger pangs – worse now that food had been so close – and the ache in his shoulders from the tight restraints. *Whatever she's planning, it's time to get ready. Although, given her clumsy attempt to steal the knife last night, there isn't much hope there. We may not get another chance before reaching the main camp.*

Hours passed. Using another jagged shard from tonight's ruined dinner, Kamin made progress on the rope at his neck, moving slowly and deliberately. The guards didn't pay any attention to him.

Although he would have liked the soldiers to be distracted from his own escape attempt, Kamin was glad Nima wasn't forced to provide another after-dinner dance tonight. Much as he'd enjoyed the performance, it wasn't worth the risk of tempting a camp full of frustrated soldiers to mutiny. Maybe the officer had reached the same conclusion after last night's dance.

As time passed with no visible repercussions to those who had eaten the dinner, Kamin grew impatient, a little angry at having his hopes raised, apparently for nothing. *But this rope is getting looser. I'll be able to make my own break for it well before dawn at this rate.* And then he'd have to decide what to do about rescuing her.

The moon was high in the sky, big and luminous, when the first man—a guard standing by the line of horses—dropped his spear and tumbled to the ground like a tree falling. Kamin tried to assess the man's condition from a distance. *Dead, I hope.* Another soldier hastened toward his fallen comrade, but his steps grew wavering and uncertain, and he, too, collapsed. All around the camp's perimeter, men now lay sprawled on the ground.

Kamin contemplated the flaps of the captain's tent, willing Nima to appear. He had no idea how long they might have. *Hurry, girl.* Impatience thrummed through his veins, and he pulled at the ropes binding him.

A small patrol had left the oasis, going into the desert for some reason and, try as he might, he couldn't remember if they'd eaten her treacherous stew before setting out. If not, those men would rejoin the column by daybreak. Sawing faster at his bonds, Kamin felt the skein unraveling. *Legs next, then retrieve a knife from one of the fallen soldiers to slash the rope on my wrists, and the odds will definitely be in my favor.* He focused on the tent flap again. *Your scheming will be for naught, little dancer, if you don't get out here. Now.*

A flicker of movement caught his eye. Holding his breath, Kamin stilled, poised for action. A moment later, Nima ran out, a knife in her hand. Sprinting straight to him, she slashed the partially cut rope at his neck, then the one binding his wrists. "Hurry," she said, reversing the knife with a skillful flick of her wrist and handing it to him. "Meet me at the horses."

He sawed at the ropes on his legs, which had been intricately knotted at his knees and ankles. *I don't need her to tell me we've got to move fast.*

Alarm spiked through his body as a yell sounded from across the camp. A Hyksos soldier stood there, gazing at the scene in disbelief. Redoubling his attack on the ropes, Kamin wondered where the man had come from, why he was conscious. The enemy soldier drew his sword and ran toward Kamin, shouting curses.

Abandoning the ropes, still hobbled at the knees and ankles, Kamin prepared to defend himself as best he could with just the knife. The man swung the sword around his head, blade whistling through the air, preparing to decapitate Kamin. Suddenly, the Hyksos grunted and stumbled, momentum driving him forward to collapse heavily on top of Kamin, despite the latter's effort to roll out of the way.

Shoving the body aside, Kamin brushed a knife buried hilt-deep in the soldier's back, right through the heart. Amazed, he raised his eyes to find the girl standing by the fire, white-faced with shock. *She threw the blade, saved my life?* Savagely slashing the last loop of rope at his ankles, Kamin surged to his feet, grabbing the loose sword as he stood. *Why isn't she moving? Is she hurt?*

She watched him stride across the campground but made no movement, other than to sway a bit. Reaching her, he realized she trembled from head to toe, probably frozen in horror at the results of her own actions.

"No regrets, you had to do it. He would have killed me," he whispered, patting her shoulder. "You made a lucky throw."

She nodded, taking a ragged breath. "Not—not luck. My step brothers taught me to throw but I've never actually—" Words choking in her throat, she swallowed hard.

"We've got to move," he said, taking her by the elbow and breaking into a run, forcing her to keep up. "Are the others dead?"

"No, the goddess didn't provide death-dealing plants. The old garden here had herbs I could use to make men sleep but not die, especially not diluted in stew." Breaking free of his grasp, she ran to grab a knife from an unconscious soldier, slipping it into the cord serving her as a belt.

Good idea. She has excellent instincts. Kamin stripped a shield from the same soldier, then they sprinted together to the horse line.

She'd already gotten one horse hitched to a chariot before coming to check on him. Kamin set the sword and shield in the vehicle and grabbed the halter of another horse. "Where did you learn to harness teams?"

Nima was following the horse line now, loosening the straps holding the animals to the tether and flapping her arms to make them shy and bolt. She frowned over her shoulder at him. "My family travels by oxcart. I figured ox, horse, four legs, not much difference." Impatiently, she shoved at a horse nibbling her sleeve. "These damn animals won't move."

"Leave them, there's no time. It's a solid plan, but we can't help it if the horses refuse to bolt." He checked the straps she had fastened and found everything in order and tight. Glancing into the chariot, he was relieved to find a war bow strapped to the side and a full quiver of arrows, then turned to see what the girl was doing. Nima was running at him, a soldier's cloak in her arms. Holding the reins, he stepped into the chariot and offered her his hand.

Glancing at his nearly naked body, she thrust the cloak at him. "You'll get cold. I grabbed one for myself as well."

Taking a second to impatiently fling the cloak over his shoulders and fasten the clasp, he set the horses off in a full gallop, rolling into the desert away from the small oasis.

"I made sure we had water, if you're thirsty," she told him, gripping the rail as the chariot sped along over the uneven ground. "I know they hardly gave you any today. There was nothing I could do about it, I'm sorry. Oh, and bread, I brought a loaf as well."

He gave her a quick, admiring glance. "You have all the contingencies covered."

She shrugged, gazing off at the desert, long straight hair flying in the breeze. "Where are we heading?"

"For now, in the opposite direction from the patrol the officer sent out earlier in the evening." Kamin applied the whip lightly to the horses. *Don't want to wear them out too soon.* "Did those soldiers eat your remarkable stew before they left camp?"

"Unfortunately, no. Amarkash was anxious for them to be gone, whatever their errand was. But I promised to keep the kettle simmering for stragglers." She shot him a mischievous glance. "I don't think they'll be eating it now, do you?"

He laughed. "Probably not. My name is Kamin, by the way. Thank you for saving my life." *Inadequate words for what she did tonight but...*

"I couldn't leave you there," she answered, eyebrows drawn together in a frown. "But we still have a long way to go to count our escape as successful."

Surprised, Kamin glanced at her. "You've a level head for someone who's been through what you've endured. How long were you with the Hyksos?"

"I lost track of time." Keeping one hand locked tightly on the railing, she raised the other to her hair, smoothing it from her face. "Five days, maybe? An eternity."

Five days of hell, no doubt. Having no idea what to say, Kamin paid full attention to driving the chariot.

*****

He drove with consummate skill, avoiding obstacles she couldn't even see in the moonlight, coaxing their best speed out of the tired animals. Nima held her cloak more closely and craned her neck to check their back trail for signs of pursuit. *I was so afraid the drugged stew wouldn't work.* Small tremors passed through her frame, and she had to keep her jaw clenched so her teeth wouldn't chatter. *I killed someone tonight.* No matter how many times she repeated the fact to herself, she couldn't quite believe she'd actually committed the deed.

When her stepbrothers taught her knife skills, they'd made her swear if she ever actually needed to defend herself, she'd throw to kill. And she had, but the wet smacking sound as the knife had struck home had been awful. Knowing she'd taken a life, even an enemy's, was a heavy weight on her heart. *But Kamin agreed I did the necessary thing. He's a soldier. He knows what's honorable.*

Racing over a small incline, the chariot jolted as it landed on the other side. To keep her from being knocked out of the chariot, Kamin grabbed her close to him with his free arm.

"I'm going to have to give the horses a break, let them walk for a few minutes," he said, his lips next to her ear. "They're tiring."

Biting her lip, she nodded, every nerve in her body screaming at the idea of slowing their headlong dash for freedom. Her head ached from the tension. "If you say we must."

"They'll run till they die otherwise. If I conserve their strength we'll get farther," he said, slowing the team gradually until the horses were walking, then pulled them to a stop. "I'm going to get out and lead them. You stay here, sit on the end of the chariot and rest. Your weight adds nothing to their burden."

She did as he suggested for a few moments, dangling her legs off the tail of the chariot while he walked at the lead horse's head, firmly holding the reins. Restless, she hopped off the vehicle and joined him, slipping into a little series of pirouettes, twirling and admiring the starry sky. *So good to be free!*

"Your dance last night was a thing of beauty," he said as she matched her stride to his.

"I'm a dancer. Dancing is what I do. I would have preferred not to give them the benefit of a performance, but Amarkash insisted." Nima glanced at him for a moment, nervously playing with a strand of her hair, then studying the ground. "Sometimes when I dance for an audience I don't care for, I stare above their heads. Or I'll pick the friendliest face in the crowd." *Should I tell him the truth?* "Last night, I was dancing for you alone."

"I'm flattered." Grinning, he shot her a sideways glance.

The promptness of his reply pleased her, and Nima laughed. "Well, don't be too flattered—you were the only Egyptian there. I gave an awful performance, merging steps from several dances, trying to avoid anything too provocative."

"I surmised you were improvising. Revising as you perform while keeping the dance flowing takes great skill. My compliments."

Nima lowered her eyes modestly for a moment. "You're a discriminating audience, not like the farmers and small-town merchants in Hebenar, may their souls gain the Afterlife."

"Was Hebenar where you were taken prisoner?" Kamin asked, his voice low and soft.

She nodded, a lump in her throat. Her chest felt tight, and tears gathered in her eyes. *I can't talk about it, not yet. I'd probably weep hysterically, and we don't have time for me to indulge myself.* "Is the team rested enough yet? I want to get as far away from the Hyksos as we can."

Kamin ran his hand over the nearest horse's neck. "I'm as impatient as you are, but these animals are our best chance to make our escape successful."

For a few moments they walked in silence, the only sound the thud of the horses' hooves on the hard ground. Bending to snatch a wildflower from its stem, he handed the fragrant little bloom to her with a flourish. "Since I have no gold of valor available, let this show my admiration for your quick thinking and bravery tonight."

"I'm suitably honored, sir," she answered, tucking the tiny yellow flower into her hair, behind her ear. *He's not like any other soldier I've ever met, not in any tavern along the Nile.* She pointed at the reins in his hand. "Are you a charioteer?"

He laughed. "No, why do you ask?"

"You drove so well, even with an unfamiliar team and this heavy chariot. You *are* a soldier?"

"I suppose my scars give away my profession."

Her stomach rumbled, startling her. "Would you like some bread?" she asked, walking to get herself a snack from the provisions bag strapped to the chariot.

"Indeed, and a long drink of water, as you promised. I'm parched. Wasting the savory dinner you cooked tonight was torture." He grinned. "You could teach the Hyksos a thing or two about torture."

Hopping into the chariot, she grabbed a piece of stale bread from the covered pannier. "Catch!" She pitched the bread at him, admiring his athleticism as he plucked the crust from the air one-handed. Preparing to rejoin Kamin, Nima glanced at the horizon while she unhooked the water skin. Lowering the container without drinking a drop, unable to keep her voice from wobbling, she said, "Set's teeth, what's this cloud of dust behind us? Can they be coming after us already? I'd hoped my potion would leave them sleeping till well after the dawn."

With one shaking finger she indicated a visible column of dust against the clear night sky behind them. Eyes narrowed, he gestured for her to get into the chariot. "Now it's going to be a race. Hold on tight." He jumped into the vehicle on her heels and flicked the reins hard, jolting their team into a gallop.

The horses flew over the ground as Kamin applied the long whip. Nima kept watch behind them and was dismayed to see the cloud of dust drawing closer, until she could make out the chariots full of soldiers.

"Three chariots, a total of seven men," she reported, tugging on Kamin's arm gently.

He risked a lightning glance behind them, his face grim. "Can you drive?"

Panic flared in Nima's gut, but she forced her voice to frame words, trying to seem confident. "Yes. I've driven oxen. Can't be terribly different."

He guffawed, a welcome sound in this tense moment. "I must meet these oxen of yours, since they apparently rival the best Hyksos chariot horses. Keep the team galloping in a straight line, unless you have to avoid an obstacle."

Swallowing hard, she edged closer to the center front of the chariot. Kamin cracked the whip again, gaining a small spurt of speed from the horses, and handed her the leather straps. Sidling over a step or two in the heaving chariot, he pulled the war bow off its hooks, grabbing an arrow from the leather quiver. He took an archer's stance next to her, aiming at their pursuers. Muscles flexing, he pulled the bow impossibly taut, wood creaking under the strain, and let the arrow fly.

"Missed," he said, selecting his next arrow.

"How can you even see well enough to aim? Isn't the chariot an unsteady platform?" She risked a quick sideways glance at him. "Should you waste the arrows?"

Shaking his head, he grinned at her, his teeth white in the moonlight. "Such doubt for my abilities. Rest assured, I'm used to shooting from a speeding chariot. Now I have the range, and the ranks of our pursuers are about to be diminished." Drawing the bow again, he let fly. Nima craned her head slightly and saw someone fall out of the pursuing chariot.

"One down," he said. "I'll even the odds for us, I promise."

His next arrow was equally deadly. Nima fought with the reins, arms pulled nearly from their sockets trying to keep the horses moving full speed in the direction Kamin wanted to go. His fourth arrow went wild as the chariot took an unexpected bounce over a ridge in the hard-packed ground.

"Sorry," Nima yelled. The gait of the horse on the left was becoming less smooth, and he stumbled. She was preparing to warn Kamin of the problem when the animal collapsed in a boneless heap and the chariot slewed, tipping on one wheel. Flying through the air, Nima instinctively tucked into an acrobat's pose, hitting the ground hard but rolling. Breath knocked out of her, she skidded and lay dazed, mouth open as she tried to suck air into her chest.

"Are you all right?" Kamin ran to her, kneeling by her side and running his hands over her body rapidly before helping her sit. "No broken bones, thank the gods. Come on, we only have moments before they arrive."

Picking her up effortlessly, he sprinted to the overturned chariot.

She wrapped her arms around his neck. "I'm sorry, I'm sorry."

"It's not your fault. We pushed the poor beast beyond his endurance." Kamin set her on her feet next to the chariot. The horse was sprawled motionless in the traces, cross tree shattered, the other horse long gone into the night. Taking a step or two, Nima knelt beside the animal's body and smoothed her palm down its neck. "Thank you," she whispered.

Putting his hand under her elbow, Kamin pulled her to her feet, giving her a gentle push toward the chariot. "Quickly, crawl under there and stay put. They won't be able to get at you without fighting their way through me, and I won't die easily."

Hearing the whooping war cries of the Hyksos warriors, Nima scrutinized the oncoming chariots. "Four to one? Kamin, you can't possibly—"

He stopped her with a kiss, tugging her body against his for a brief moment, his heat warming her chilled limbs before she pushed him away, wiping her lips.

Kamin laughed. "If I'm fighting for a beautiful girl like you, I can. And they want us alive, remember? Now get under there."

Dropping to her knees, she crawled as far under the chariot as she could get. It wasn't much in the way of shelter, but it was at least better than standing in the open, where the enemy could outflank Kamin and seize her. *If I could be any help to him, I wouldn't be hiding in here.* Nima drew the knife from her belt and held it at the ready. She swallowed hard, fingers clenched around the carved bone hilt. *When—if—the enemy gets past Kamin, I'm not surrendering.* The knife would find her heart.

Leaning forward she peered through the opening. The Hyksos chariots pulled up with a great flourish, but Kamin skewered one of their number through the heart with his last arrow, before dropping the bow and drawing the sword. Shield in one hand, blade in the other, he took a warrior's defensive position, right side toward the enemy, knees slightly bent, weight centered, and waited for them to come to him.

The drivers stayed with their chariots, leaving two Hyksos to carry the attack to Kamin. With a great yell and an oath, Kamin charged forward, taking them by surprise. Nima gasped as he slashed the sword arm of the first man, nearly severing it, and then moved in a blur to parry the stroke the second soldier made. He and the enemy fought desperately on the hard-packed earth in front of the chariot. Kamin sliced the other man's round, wooden shield in half and barely missed decapitating him as his opponent made a fluid sidestep, saving himself. Heart pounding, Nima watched as Kamin pursued his advantage, raining powerful slashes on the other man's broken shield and sword, fighting with intensity and total concentration. The Hyksos could barely manage to stave off the assault as Kamin drove him to one knee. She'd never seen actual mortal combat, and the violence and speed of the blows were terrifying.

Only the young officer was left on his feet, visibly reluctant to engage in combat. He had his sword drawn but stayed on the sidelines, yelling instructions at his soldier as the man tried to fend off Kamin's assault. He took tentative steps toward the two combatants but hesitated and raised his shield even though Kamin wasn't making any moves in his direction.

Yet.

In his death throes, the soldier fell. A bloodstained Kamin, baring his teeth in a feral grin, whirled to face the officer.

Swallowing hard, the young Hyksos lifted his blade as Kamin advanced. "So, it seems you're not just a craven spy, Egyptian. You have some fighting skills. Be warned, for I'm an officer, trained by the best in our army."

Laughing, Kamin swung a massive blow against the man's upraised shield, easily parrying the man's first slash, forcing him into a stumbling retreat. "Brave words, Hyksos, too bad your training yielded such paltry results!"

Not much of a contest there. Easy prey for Kamin. A furtive movement drew Nima's attention to the two remaining chariot drivers. One was on the ground, setting an arrow to his bow, waiting for an opening to shoot Kamin and cripple him.

"Oh, no, you don't," she said through her teeth, slithering forward in the dirt to leave her shelter.

As she stood to throw her knife, the two drivers spotted her. The archer retargeted, but before he could release the bow string, she'd launched her deadly weapon, hurling it with all the force in her body. The blade buried itself in his heart. A surprised expression on his face, he toppled over, the arrow skittering wildly across the ground. The other driver cursed her in torrents of Hyksos. Frantically, he tied off the reins he held, linking the two chariot teams head to head so they couldn't wander off while he pursued her.

Nima sprinted to the nearest dead soldier, pawing through his cloak. *He must have a knife—where is it?* Grabbed from behind, she was yanked to her feet, the soldier trying to get a firm grip and subdue her.

"Egyptian bitch, you'll be punished for this day's work," he muttered in her ear. "And I'll enjoy watching."

Kicking at his shins, she bit his arm, taking advantage of his momentary flinch to wrench herself free. Yelling a battle cry, Kamin came running and cut the last Hyksos down on the spot.

Breathing hard, dizzy, Nima sank to her knees. Kamin, splattered with blood, wounded in the arm and leg, glared at her, his own chest heaving like a bellows.

He checked the area with one rapid glance, then dropped the sword and shield to kneel beside her.

"Didn't I tell you to stay under the chariot?" His voice was thick with anger, but his eyes betrayed his concern for her. "Are you hurt?"

Numb, she shook her head, reaching out to touch the edge of his arm wound. "The cowards were going to shoot you in the back. I couldn't stay hidden—I had to do something. We need to clean and bandage your wounds."

"Not now, there's no time. We've got to keep going. Amarkash will send more patrols out in the daylight. We have to find a safe place to hole up and rest, plan our next steps." He pulled off the cloak and ripped two pieces from the hem, holding them out to her. "Can you do a temporary bandage?"

She wound the first strip firmly around his arm, but not too tight, tying it off with a neat knot. The other slash was on his thigh, right below his loincloth, and she hesitated a moment. Taking the cloth from her gently, Kamin wrapped his own leg, giving her a sideways glance but not saying anything. He clenched his teeth as he made the bandage tight.

Nima scrambled to her feet, dusting off her skirt. "Which chariot shall we take, then? Do you have a preference?" She walked over to the tethered teams and patted the neck of the nearest horse.

"Actually," he said, retrieving the sword and shield, then walking slowly after her, "I thought we might take a gamble."

"A gamble?" Nima bent to the knotted reins lying on the ground, sitting cross-legged to untie the straps for whatever he suggested next.

Joining her, he took the reins she had unknotted. "Are you a betting woman?"

What a reckless gleam he gets in his eyes—impossible to resist. "I can be. I play a wicked game of senet."

He mimicked rolling dice. "I'll have to challenge you one day, when we have more time. For now, I was thinking we might send both chariots on their way, in different directions, create two false trails for our pursuers to follow while we hike to those sandstone cliffs over there." He pointed to the east.

Pivoting on her heel, Nima tried to estimate how much hiking would be required to reach the distant cliffs. "Can we get there by dawn, do you think? Distances are deceiving out here. And what about the injury to your leg?"

"My leg will be fine. Just a cut. " Taking a step, he gave her shoulder a gentle squeeze of reassurance. "We'll make it, I promise. And I'm sure from the look of the canyons ahead, we'll find a cave for us to shelter in."

"All right." She gathered her cloak and followed him to the tethered chariots. They rummaged through the baskets and pouches, taking as much water and food as they could carry. Kamin acquired a new, more powerful bow and a leather quiver full of arrows, which he slung across one shoulder before untying the ground hitch and setting both teams of horses bolting with a crack of the whip.

"Now." He dropped the whip beside their upended vehicle and took Nima by the elbow. "We go as fast as we can in the opposite direction."

The trip to the cliffs was a blur for Nima. She couldn't imagine how Kamin stayed so strong with his wounds, minor though he insisted they were, as well as the debilitating effects of two days of forced march as a prisoner. They ran, slowed to a walk and then ran again. Kamin had taken the majority of the supplies to carry, but even the small water skin she'd slung on her back felt like a boulder by the time they stood at the base of the stone formation.

The sun was rising slowly, casting long shadows out into the desert behind them.

"Rest," Kamin ordered her as he stripped off the supplies and weapons. "Have a seat on this convenient rock and wait while I find us a cave."

Suddenly afraid to be left alone, she held the rough fabric of his cloak tight in her fist. "What if they come while you're gone?"

He met her eyes, his face serious but calm. "They won't, I promise you. If Amarkash sent any more patrols out last night, they'll be chasing the empty chariots. I don't want you scrambling around in the rocks until I know where we're going."

She released her grip on the cloak and walked over to the perch he'd indicated, lifting herself onto the flat top. "Don't be gone too long, all right?"

"I give you my word." He made a half bow and was gone, working his way deeper into the narrow canyon.

CHAPTER TWO

When he eventually returned, Nima sat where he'd left her, wrapped in her cloak and watching the trail for any sign of pursuit. As tumbling pebbles from the incline above announced Kamin's arrival, she spun around on the boulder, wide-eyed and gasping.

"All clear out there?" he asked, shading his eyes with his hand and gazing across the wide expanse they'd recently traveled.

"I think so. I hope so." She shoved the dagger into her belt and flipped her long braid over her shoulder, then slid off the rock into his arms. "Did you find us a place to rest?"

"A snug little cave, with its own stream running down the middle. Can you guess the best part?" He helped her steady herself and then stepped away. She's such a petite armful. Desire swept through his body. Willing himself to think of something other than Nima, he headed for the small stack of provisions and weapons. *Control yourself. After being brutalized by the Hyksos, I'm sure she's not in the mood for* me *to make advances.* He collected the water and provisions while she leaned on the boulder.

He held out his hand, and she put her slender fingers into his, letting him lead her for the first few feet up the trail, saying as she hiked, "I know nothing about caves. What's so pleasing, then?"

"No occupants to battle us for possession of the space." He half lifted her over the first boulder on the path. "If you can handle a few minutes of climbing, we'll be there. Today you can rest in safety, if not much comfort."

The climb wasn't too arduous, and Kamin was constantly at her elbow to assist her as needed, ensuring she didn't fall.

"You climb well for a novice," he said after they'd navigated a particularly steep gorge. *The gods couldn't have sent me a better partner for this mad escape. Another soldier wouldn't have been able to free us the way she did. Few women could maintain the pace as she does.*

Hands on hips, Nima paused to take a few deep breaths. "Dancer, remember? Strong legs, excellent balance."

Oh, yes, I have no problem at all remembering you're a dancer, with those beautiful legs. Now is not the time for me to think about your legs. Closing his eyes for a second at the mental picture of those shapely limbs wrapped around him, holding him close as he buried his cock in her warmth, Kamin moved up the hill, berating himself. *Where's my self-control? This woman has far too much of an effect on me for the dangerous situation we're in.* "The cave is after the next bend, not much farther."

When they reached the grotto, she ducked under the ledge and stretched with a sigh of pleasure. "Spacious indeed," she said. "A palace among caves."

"Refresh yourself with a drink from the stream. The water's cold and pure."

Nima knelt and washed her face, then drank from her cupped hands while he deposited their supplies against the far wall.

Pointing to a large, fallen slab next to the cave wall, he said, "I suggest you rest here. I'm going to drag some bushes in front of the entrance, hide us from view, in case any Hyksos wander nearby."

"I should make something to eat," she protested, drying her face and hands on the edge of her skirt.

"We can't risk a fire. Much as I'd enjoy tasting whatever you could cook from our small store of rations, I can take care of myself. You need to rest. You've been running on nervous energy all night." He surveyed her from head to toe. "Probably since the Hyksos captured you, yes?"

Grimacing, Nima rubbed her hand over her lower legs. "How did you know? Aches and pains I've been ignoring are prodding me for attention."

He walked over to spread his cloak on the large, flat rock. "Sit here. Relax. I'm only sorry I can't make it into a luxurious couch, soft and cozy."

"I'll manage." Grabbing one of the small sacks, she wadded it up to serve as a crude pillow.

He pointed at her red, lacerated wrists. "After I've created some camouflage, I want to examine those rope burns for you, clean them at least."

"And I need to bandage your injuries for you." Yawning, she rubbed her eyes. "If I fall asleep, wake me, all right?"

With serious reservations, Kamin nodded. *If she can sleep under these conditions, I'm not going to rouse her to take care of me.* Pausing, he watched her lean her head against the wall, cushioned by the sack, and close her eyes. Only when her breathing had evened out and he was sure she was asleep did he go outside to construct his camouflage wall.

*****

Cherry-colored flames with yellow and violet cores crackling everywhere, above and below. The blackened roof timbers groaned, glowing from the inside out. How much longer would they hold? Small pieces were falling away each moment, burning embers igniting new blazes wherever they fell. Wind generated by the fire itself blew sparks in a mad whirl.

Her skin hot, dry as the desert to the point of pain. *I'm baking alive.*

The screams from every direction had stopped or were muffled by the roaring flames. She couldn't stay where she was, but if she broke cover and ran, the attackers would see her. The hem of her dress smoldered where an ember landed with a hiss, catching fire. Hurriedly, she beat it out, but the heat was too intense and the noxious black smoke was choking her. *Give up, stay here and die, anything is better than being captured.* But even as she tried to convince herself, her body was moving frantically, instinctively, to find air and relief from the fire. Shielding her head with her arms, she ran into the hall, crouching low to breathe. She sprawled full length over a body in the corridor.

Scrambling to her knees as a portion of the ceiling collapsed behind her, Nima scrabbled her way to the stairs. The entire upper floor exploded into a solid sheet of flames. She threw herself down the stairs, slithering on her belly in a mad rush, crouching as low as she could when she fell off the bottom riser.

Avoiding several more corpses in the main room of the inn, she frantically brushed embers out of her hair. Weaving a path between smoldering columns, crawling at some points, she tried to orient herself in the inferno. *Find the door.* The place she knew so well was now an unrecognizable scene from hell. It was as if the legendary lake of fire, where demons and condemned souls lived, had somehow poured through the inn's doors and windows.

Chest burning and constricted, coughing so deeply her ribs ached, Nima burst out of the burning inn, dodging a falling beam at the doorway. She staggered a few more steps, drawing in deep, gasping breaths of the cool night air as she fell to her knees. Suddenly, she was seized from behind by a laughing Hyksos soldier, who lifted her like a child and spun her to face him.

"We expected you'd come out eventually, rather than burn to death, dancer," he jeered, mouth next to her lips as he pawed at her scorched linen dress, ripping the neckline and exposing her breasts.

Screaming, Nima clawed his face with her nails. A second man crowded behind her, his aroused cock pressing urgently against her bottom, his hands raising her dress past her thighs, while the first soldier caressed her. The two men were forcing her to the ground despite her terrified resistance, other soldiers gathering to participate, touching her, restraining her. Her vision was going black. Thunder crashed as the inn fell—

No, it was a steady heartbeat under her ear, strong arms holding her reassuringly, not groping. She was pressed to a broad chest, a soothing voice murmuring soft words to her in crisp Egyptian, not growling Hyksos. Trying to calm her breathing, she let the words pour over her shattered nerves while the immediate terror of the dream receded.

"Easy, easy, shh, Nima, you're here with me now. No harm will come to you, I promise. Wake up, shake off the dream world. Open your eyes, see you're safe. Remember, we escaped together? I promised no harm would come to you."

Nima concentrated on the deep, reassuring voice promising protection, drawing her out of the nightmare. Taking a shuddering breath, she opened her eyes, realizing she was safe in Kamin's arms.

Relieved to see her emerging from the grip of the nightmare, he loosened his embrace the moment she made a slight movement to put distance between them. Gently, he stroked his hand through her hair, rubbed her back in circles. Shudders racked her body.

"You were screaming so loud your throat must be raw," he said. "I couldn't wake you."

"I was in the flames, the inn burning. And then the men attacking me—" She caught her breath on a huge sob.

Gods, what an ordeal she's been through. Kamin quelled his automatic response to her, his desire for her, which was nigh impossible with her sitting across his thighs. *But she wouldn't wake up no matter what I did, she was fighting the terrors of the dream so desperately.* "I'm sorry you had to go through the ordeal. I wish I'd been there to defend you."

An edge of hysteria sharpened her laugh. "Amarkash came and reprimanded the soldiers, made them stop before they'd done more than frighten and bruise me. He said they had their orders, to treat me as untouchable, meant for someone else."

"For himself," Kamin said with fury, grinding his teeth. "The bastard."

She shook her head. "No, he didn't assault me either, thank the gods. He—he enjoyed inflicting pain. He enjoyed tying me up each night, describing awful things his general was going to do to me when we reached their fortress, but he didn't go any further."

"His general?" Kamin's brow was furrowed. "He kidnapped you for someone else?" *Odd behavior, even for a Hyksos.*

Wiping away a few lingering tears, Nima sniffed. "Apparently, the Hyksos had been to the village before, and several others in the area, and had seen me dance. My family travels through the Shield of Egypt province giving shows."

Nodding, Kamin said, "The Hyksos have been studying this nome. I can easily believe they traveled the province in disguise to gain information on their targets before attacking."

Nima blotted the moisture on her face with her sleeve. "Well, this general apparently gave strict orders I was to be captured at all costs and brought to him. Untouched."

She took a deep breath, holding it as Kamin tilted her face gently, studying the faded bruises. Anger flared hot in his gut. "Among other unfortunate things, he left the definition of untouched to Amarkash. Let me get the wineskin. I think a drink would calm your nerves."

Setting her gently on a rock ledge, he rose to get the wine. He'd bathed, rewrapped his own wounds, and donned a coarsely woven, brown-striped Hyksos kilt while she'd slept.

"I was supposed to take care of your injuries," she protested when he came to sit down, touching the bandage on his arm lightly with her fingertips.

He glanced at his arm as he worked to uncork the wineskin. "I'm perfectly capable of doing field dressings."

"I don't drink wine normally." She pulled away as he offered her the wineskin. "I have to keep a level head when I'm dancing for a crowd in a tavern."

"Trust me, you'll benefit from it today. A few sips, to please me?" He grinned. "There won't be any dancing. I'm not trying to get you drunk, only take the edge off your nerves."

"I wasn't concerned about you trying to get me drunk," she said with offended dignity. Drinking two quick swallows, she pushed the wineskin firmly away, slight tremors weakening her a bit. "I don't like to lose control to the wine."

When she dropped her head against his shoulder, her hair covered him like a soft blanket.

"You're shaking," he said, rubbing her arm. "Are you warm enough?"

Nima braided a plait of hair and then unbraided it. "I can't get the nightmare out of my mind, much less the terror of the actual events. So many people dead, slaughtered. And the other young women weren't as lucky as I was. Amarkash took me to his chariot, but I—I had to watch and hear what was done to the others. The women and the children and a few of the men who survived were sold as slaves to a slave master waiting outside town."

Kamin covered her restless hands with one of his, curling his fingers around hers, rubbing his thumb along the edge of her hand. "What about your family?"

"They were away, performing at the name day celebration for a local noble's wife. I pretended to be ill so I could remain behind."

"Why didn't you want to go with them?" He took a swig of the wine himself.

She closed her eyes. "It's a long story."

"We've endless hours of daylight ahead of us since we don't dare travel till nightfall. I'm a good listener," he said, taking another short drink then capping the wineskin decisively. "Unless you think you could sleep?"

Half-braided hair flying, she shook her head, opening her eyes wide and putting a hand to her forehead. "The dream is waiting, like a lion about to pounce."

"Well, then, distract us both with a story about the most beautiful dancer in Shield of Egypt province, handy with knives and poisonous herbs, who took pity on a poor soldier and rescued him." He raised his eyebrows.

"Sounds like a scribe's tale for children when you describe the events of the past few days in such fashion." Kamin was gratified to see a slight smile on her lips as she responded to his playful tone. "It wasn't nearly as amusing to live through," Nima said.

"How is it you know about knives and herbs anyway?" he asked. "Hardly the usual training for dancers where I come from."

Nima fingered the amulet on her left wrist. "My mother was a disgraced priestess, from a small temple. I don't know where."

Curious, he tried to identify which goddess might value dancing and knife-wielding assassins. Kamin frowned. "Which Great One did she serve? I myself am sworn to Horus."

"I don't know. She died when I was young, and she never spoke of her life before, at least not to me." With a dancer's flourish, she held out her wrist. "This is my only clue about the goddess."

Holding her hand carefully in his much bigger one, Kamin examined the single glazed oval bead, about two inches long, threaded on a simple black leather thong, knotted loosely to circle her wrist. Pale aqua green in color, the flat bead under the glaze had a partial hieroglyphic on one side and a raised, snakelike design on the other, with two tiny enameled flowers flanking the reptile's head. "Nothing I recognize. Renenutet, the snake goddess, maybe? These resemble mountain flowers, so maybe a local deity related to the supreme snake goddess?"

"Who can say? I believe this bead was part of a longer necklace at some time. I think my mother kept it from her happier days in the temple. When I was a baby, she gave it to me as an amulet, but she never uttered the name of the Great One. She told me it might bring the goddess to me in a time of need, but only once, so I wasn't to use the gift lightly. When she was banished from the ranks of temple dancers, she apparently begged, not for herself, but for this one future favor on my behalf." Nima squinted at the bead for a moment, rotating it on the thong with her fingertips. "Amarkash said it was worthless clay, so he left it alone." She tapped the snake with one fingernail. "The amulet's never brought me luck. It's never brought me anything but comfort in the knowledge my mother loved me. Certainly no goddess came to help when the Hyksos captured me." Eyes cast down, she blinked away a tear. "I don't even know who my father was. Some rich and careless noble who abandoned her is what the troupe members told me, but I don't know the truth."

A bleak tale. My own family frustrates me at times, but at least we know we belong to each other. And I resemble my father in all respects, gods grant he rests well in the Afterlife. Kamin assessed Nima's condition. She was still too pale, her body racked by occasional tremors, eyes unseeing. *Time for more distracting conversation.* "But you refer to the performers as your family?"

"My mother was a trained temple dancer, so after she was banished, she sought to make her living in the taverns, and this troupe took her—us—in." Nima shrugged. "I was just a baby, so I don't remember our life before we joined Dudekh and Gamisis and their players."

"When you started dancing the other night, at the Hyksos camp, I was sure you must be a temple dancer," he told her. "You had the classical movements perfectly."

Her blush was enchanting, color flowing into her pale cheeks. "Thank you. Serving a goddess by dancing for her pleasure, living safe and secure in a temple, would be a dream, but I perform in the taverns and street fairs instead." Nima put her head against his shoulder. "My mother drowned in the Nile when I was seven. I've always wondered if she walked to the riverbank planning to die. She was so unhappy."

"But the performers gave you a home?" He tried to keep doubt out of his tone. *Such people are not known for their charity. And they don't extend themselves to outsiders without good reason.*

Her next words confirmed his opinion. "Not out of true kindness. I dance better than any of them, and they know it." A strong note of pride rang in her voice. "I inherited my mother's gift, and she trained me intensively before she died. The noble who hired the troupe on the night of the Hyksos's attack was probably angry I didn't come. Dudekh would insist I couldn't be hired separately. The whole family had to be employed."

"So they used you as bait to line their pockets?" *What a life of drudgery and sadness she's had.*

"Yes." She sighed. "As I got older and stopped seeing through a child's eyes, I realized they were not nice people."

"You said they taught you to throw knives?"

"And brew poisons and potions, cheat at senet, pick pockets—" Counting the skills off on her fingers, she enumerated the unusual list wryly.

She had a triumphant little grin on her face. *Gods, I want to kiss her. Her lips fascinate me, but now is not the time.*

Apparently unaware of his inner struggle over his body's reaction to her, Nima snuggled closer.

"And I'm grateful, especially for your skill with cooking poisonous stews," he assured her. "But why didn't you go with the troupe to the noble's celebration?"

Not meeting his eyes, she traced an intricate pattern in her skirt with one finger. "I feigned illness because I had been thinking for a while of running away from them. The night of the noble's festivities seemed like my chance, only I was afraid to actually set out alone, unprotected."

Kamin pursued the thought. "But what had changed about living and traveling with them? Why did you want to run away?"

"Dudekh's old crone of a wife, Gamisis, kept pushing me to give private dances, as the other girls did, for men who could pay her for the privilege. I'm convinced that's what the noble wanted." Nima grimaced. "Although if I'd gone, the Hyksos wouldn't have captured me. Maybe I should have given in to Gamisis."

His arms tightened around her. "I swear to you, soldier's oath, you aren't going back to those people. When we get out of this predicament, once the Hyksos fortress has been destroyed—"

"A person has to have deben to live," she said simply. "I need a roof, food, clothing, like anyone else. At least the troupe was protection when some drunken patron wanted to touch me or was waiting after the tavern closed to proposition me. I've received several private offers from rich men, nobles, to accept their protection, join their households exclusively, but I've no desire to be someone's concubine, no matter how pleasant he may be or how good a lover. I won't be a possession, discarded when I'm too old to dance." Her voice rang with contempt. She played with the frayed hem of her dress, braiding and unbraiding the raggedy strands. "I want to be in charge of my own life, never perform again, unless for an audience of my own choosing. I want to see more of the world than the same border towns and taverns. I want to be respectably married someday, have children, be mistress of a household. " Her voice trailed off, but after a moment she shook herself and straightened. "First, I have to escape the life I'm trapped in."

Such simple dreams shouldn't be out of reach. He tilted her chin, reached to take the now-wilted flower from her ebony hair. "Well, then, we'll get the nomarch who rules this province in Pharoah's name to issue you a fat reward, genuine gold of valor, for saving my life, and you can make your way anywhere you choose." He blew the limp petals off his fingertips.

Watching the tiny fragments spiral away in the slight breeze, Nima half smiled. "You dream big, soldier."

Actually I dream of you now. Kamin took a deep breath. "Nima—"

She set her fingers on his lips. "I don't think we should tempt fate by talking of the future. We have to get all the way to Tentaris to warn the nomarch first. And then see how grateful he may be." A huge yawn overtook her. "I think the wine is making me sleepy. I told you I've no head for wine."

"Sleep then." He grabbed the makeshift pillow with his free hand and tried to plump it up against his thigh before handing it to her. "I'll be on guard, for the Hyksos or the nightmares."

"You need to rest," she answered drowsily, reclining and shoving the sack under her head. "I can take the watch for part of the time."

Adjusting his shoulders to be more comfortable, he leaned against the rock. "I'll be fine. Soldiers learn to sleep with one eye open. Have no fear."

"I'm not afraid, not with you." Eyes closing, she curled up next to him, like a cat. He had to clench his fist on his thigh to resist the urge to stroke her shining hair. For a moment or two, her soft breathing was the only sound, other than the gentle gurgling of the brook.

"Kamin?"

He brought his attention back from the stream. "Yes?"

She kept her eyes closed. "I haven't done any private dances. I've yet to meet the man I *want* to dance for."

CHAPTER THREE

A few moments before sunset, he woke her, and they made the best meal they could from the remnants of what they'd stolen from the Hyksos camp, washing it down with the cold water, before repacking their gear and climbing out of the canyon before the sun set completely.

Stomach sinking, Nima contemplated the vast expanse of sand and semi-arid desert. "How are we ever going to find our way to the city?"

"I'm a pretty fair tracker." He pointed in the direction he intended to go, and they both started walking. "We'll hike due east, opposite the setting sun, arriving on the banks of the Nile in one or two nights' travel. From there we can get a boat or maybe even a chariot, depending where we intersect the river or cross the caravan road. I can requisition transportation at any government house." He scrutinized himself, clad in a Hyksos kilt and cloak, and frowned. "I may have some trouble convincing the authorities of my identity."

"The officer called you a spy, right before you killed him," Nima said. "Are you really a spy?"

Kamin searched her face for a moment, his own serious, eyes narrowed. "Yes," he said finally. "I'll admit that much. The Hyksos have Egyptian sympathizers in this province, have even planted some of their own people in positions of power masquerading as Egyptians." He started walking as he went on. "Pharaoh needs to destroy their network, dig them out by the roots to throw them out of our country for all time."

Skipping to close the distance between them, she raised her hand peremptorily. "Better if you don't tell me the details. We might be recaptured, and I can't be made to tell what I don't know."

"You possess good sense." Plucking a long strand of grass from a hillock as he passed, he chewed on it for a moment. "But this province traveled a long way down the road to hell during the Usurper Pharaoh's reign. The Hyksos presence represents a major threat."

She frowned. *I can't even imagine trying to fool the enemy into thinking I was one of them.*

"Were you a good spy?"

"Since I got myself captured, you might think the answer is no." Kamin laughed, attractive lines crinkling at the corners of his eyes. "I was about to make a final report to the nomarch at the capital. I have all the details, all the contacts, all the traitors' names, here." He tapped his forehead lightly. "The gods blessed me with the ability to remember vast quantities of information. You recall dance steps, I remember facts."

"You'd have made an excellent scribe then," she said.

"Not likely. I'd soon lose my wits, cooped up in a counting house or a library all day."

"A scribe's life would have been safer." She scuffed at a pebble. Safety seemed a highly desirable thing to her, given their circumstances.

Hands on his hips, he stopped walking. "Do I seem like a man who craves a *safe* life to you?"

Laughing at the comic, horrified expression on his face until she couldn't breathe, Nima clutched her aching sides and said, "Don't be insulted. No, of course, you're unquestionably a man who enjoys going in harm's way. How were you captured, if not in battle?"

Kamin strolled onward. "At the last meeting I attended, there was a man who'd seen me before, in Thebes. He knew I wasn't what I claimed to be here in Nome of the Shield. Realizing he'd recognized me, I slipped out of the gathering, but I was pursued and outnumbered." Shading his eyes with one hand, Kamin stared at the horizon. "Now I need to get across this damn desert and back to civilization, so I can deliver my report."

"At least we have the rudiments of a plan," she said. "Of course, the Hyksos had a map, which would be preferable."

Kamin stopped dead in his tracks and wheeled slowly to stare at her, eyebrows raised. "A map? What kind of map?"

She kept striding along at the pace she had set for herself, passing him and continuing on. "One leading to their fortress in the mountains at the edge of the desert, of course. Amarkash consulted it constantly, day and night, checking landmarks and the alignment of the stars. Why?"

Coming after her, Kamin grabbed her arm, loosening his grip a bit as she winced. "He let you see this map? Could you reproduce it?"

"I suppose, but why? We don't want to arrive at their stronghold. I've had more than enough close encounters with the Hyksos." Bending over, she plucked an annoying twig from her sandal and tossed it away.

"No one knows where their base is. That closely guarded secret eluded even my efforts to ferret out information." Kamin threw his arms wide. "A map would be a gift from the gods. The enemy would never expect us to attack, and the nomarch's army could surprise them, destroying the whole place."

"It might be pretty well defended." Nima was dubious, pursing her lips and chewing at the interior of her cheek. "The general who sent Amarkash to kidnap me was supposed to be one of their top strategists. Nebu something."

"Set's teeth, I will be damned to the lake of fire," Kamin said, pounding his fist into his open palm. "Was his name Nebuchazz?"

"Yes." She tugged at his sleeve. "Come on, we need to keep walking."

Brow furrowed, Kamin resumed the hike, head tilted as he considered her confirmation of the man's name.

Nima frowned herself. "What difference does it make who the general is?"

Eyes sparkling at the thought, he said, "If we could kill or capture him, the Hyksos' plans to take over Egypt would be dealt a severe blow. Can you draw me this map when we stop to rest later?"

"I'll try. I have a pretty good memory. I certainly saw the parchment enough times." *Usually right before Amarkash tied me up for the night.* Nima shivered at the memory of the Hyksos officer's rough, callused hands on her body, fastening the ropes into intricate knots while he touched her in intimate places.

Lost in the terror of memory, she hadn't realized she'd stopped walking.

Reaching out, Kamin tugged at her curls. "Banish the thoughts making you hesitate. You're with me now. You're safe. I'll protect you."

She wrapped her arms around herself and rocked on her heels. "If they overtake us, I'll use the dagger on myself. I refuse to be recaptured."

He laid one hand over his heart. "I'm not going to let you be taken prisoner again, my oath on it."

Stopping to rest periodically, they walked and jogged through the night. At first, Nima believed it was an amazing coincidence when Kamin called a halt every time she was on the verge of telling him she could go no farther, but then she realized he was watching her without seeming to do so, evaluating her condition and pacing himself.

As she drank the water he handed her and nibbled at their last remaining bread crust, she admired his muscular frame, his handsome face. *But what I appreciate most is how considerate of me he's been. It's a relief – nay, a luxury - to have someone so capable, so deadly, watching over me, concerned about my comfort.* He turned in her direction, and she averted her eyes, not wishing to be caught gawking. *Could I ever mean something to him as a woman, not merely a person he's grateful to for rescuing him?* She laid her head on her knees, wistfully considering what it would be like to belong to a man like Kamin and wondering what his story was. *I told him mine.* But, of course, he was a spy, so he had to keep most things about himself secret, she supposed with a little sigh.

"So." He touched her on the shoulder, making her jump a little, as if he could read her thoughts. "Can you draw me the map now?"

"Oh, I forgot. Of course I can." Blushing, flustered, she placed the water skin on the ground and cast a puzzled glance at him. "But on what? We have no papyrus, no tablets."

He tapped his forehead lightly with his index finger. "Excellent memory. I just need you to draw it for me in the sand, then I'll have it up here. I can reproduce it on papyrus once we return to civilization." With a quick movement, he handed her his dagger, hilt first. "Your pen, my lady scribe."

She giggled at his exaggerated formality. "I'm no scribe and certainly no lady. I can read and write a few hieroglyphics, no more. I told you, my stepfather believed in practical education."

"Which stood you, and me, in good stead, although your troupe master shouldn't expect my thanks any time soon." He smoothed a patch of sandy soil between them with the palm of his hand. "Here's your slate. I think the moonlight is sufficient, thanks to the Great One Nuit's generosity."

Nima paused a moment, considering how to begin. "I've never drawn anything before." Then she outlined a neat square at the top of the sand. "This was the fortress. There were odd markings, like the building was surrounded by hills." She made delicate indentations in the sand with the tip of the knife. "And here, these are the corresponding alignments of the stars, at least at this season."

"Excellent details," Kamin approved. "Now the trail leading to it?"

Moving the knife tip to the opposite side of the sand square, she drew a smaller box. "Hebenar, the village where they caught me." She closed her eyes for a second. Even the mere act of uttering the doomed settlement's name brought sadness and horror flooding into her mind.

"Don't let the memories intrude." Lightly, Kamin squeezed her shoulder, as if they were comrades in arms. "You're here with me now, not there."

Dropping the knife into the dirt, she rubbed her hand across her eyes, furious to be tearing up again in his presence. "Will I ever be able to forget?"

He reached out and caught her to him, hugging her as she cried. "It's all right, let the tears wash away some of the fear and pain."

"I want to *forget*." Nima protested, her voice wobbly.

She could feel the motion as he shook his head. He rubbed a hand down her back in lazy circles. "I can't lie. Crying will help, but the memories won't fade completely. They dim with time, I promise."

"And—and those two men I killed?" Will I ever be able to walk away from those deeds?" She sobbed harder, weeping in deep paroxysms. "When my heart is weighed by the gods after my death, will I be judged as having done the right thing? Or will they give my *ka* to Ammit the Destroyer?"

"You didn't commit murder. You were engaged in warfare on behalf of Egypt. The gods will account for that." Kamin murmured soft words in her ear, held her close.

Nima had no idea how long she indulged herself in the emotional release, but eventually the sobs faded to sniffles and hiccups, and the tears no longer fell. *Such a luxury, to be comforted. There's no tenderness in any member of Dudekh's dance troupe.*

Kamin held her away from him enough to see her face. With one hand, he blotted the tears on her cheeks. "Better now?"

Reaching for the corner of her cloak, she spilled a tiny bit of the water onto it to wash her face. "I'm sorry to have wept all over you."

"You needed to cry." Taking the cloak, he dried a spot on her cheek she'd missed. "I hope it helped?"

"A little." She pressed one hand to her aching heart. "I was so helpless and terrified the night I was captured. Some of those people who died were friends. The town was my favorite stop on our regular route of touring, so I was thinking of trying to escape the troupe there. The innkeeper in Hebenar was always nice to me, snuck me extra food. And the two serving maids were twins, sweet girls my age. When I was in town, we used to go shopping in the bazaar together. I'd promised to dance at the older sister's wedding." Hiccupping a bit, Nima closed her eyes in pain. "She died when the soldiers were—when they had her—" Voice fading, she gulped against renewed sobs.

"If talking about the events helps you ease the memories plaguing your mind, I'll listen to the entire tale as often as you need to tell it," Kamin said, embracing her again. "Too much for you to carry alone. I have broad shoulders."

"You're so kind to me, so patient." She searched his face. "Why?"

"You saved my life, risked your own to do so." His answer was prompt and emphatic. "You could have left me there, let me eat the drugged stew along with our captors, to avoid any possibility I might betray you."

"Never!" Cutting across his words, she protested immediately. "I wouldn't have drugged you. Leaving you never even crossed my mind."

"I know," he said, patting her on the shoulder. "You've much honor. But, as I was going to say before you interrupted me, I've got three younger sisters who've needed comforting at times. Although, thank the gods, not for anything approaching what you've endured."

"Oh." *He thinks of me as a little sister?* The idea was deflating.

Studying her reaction, he frowned, hazel eyes narrowing. "Now your mind is going in the wrong direction, I fear." He caught her chin and lifted her face to his. "Because a man *has* sisters doesn't mean he sees every beautiful woman he meets *as* a sister. You have to know I find you incredibly desirable? Surely you saw how my body responded to you, how nothing else mattered to me in the moment of your dance, even though I was a prisoner in peril." He glanced away, seeming a bit embarrassed by his declaration of her effect on him. "Such is the power of your art."

She nodded a little shyly, feeling warmth bloom in her cheeks. She was glad it was night—perhaps he wouldn't observe her blush. "I—I noticed. I was pleased, although it wasn't my intent to arouse."

"Now is not the time or the place for me to pursue what I feel for you." His voice was a little rough as he stared into her eyes. "Gods willing, we're going to have the leisure and the right surroundings someday."

She blinked at his vehemence. Rising, Kamin paced away a few steps, turning to the horizon, ostensibly scanning the wide-open plains. Retrieving the dagger,

Nima renewed her efforts to complete her crude map. *Could he have not merely desire but affection for me? I think I'm falling in love with him like a foolish girl in a scribe's tale. For all I know, he has a fat wife and seven children somewhere.*

After a moment, Kamin walked over to watch her, asking questions about the markings as she drew them. Finally, she laid the knife aside and surveyed the map top to bottom, biting her lip as she concentrated. Brushing aside some loose dirt drifting across the representation of the trail, she dusted her hands off. "This is as much as I can recall, but I think it's pretty much complete."

"Amarkash was a fool. He seriously underestimated you, in all ways, thank the gods." Kamin squatted on his haunches, hands resting on his powerful thighs. "Let me have a few moments to commit this to memory, and then we'll wipe it away and get moving again."

"I'll keep watch." She stood, adjusting her blue dress, then taking up position where he'd been, eyeing the horizon in all directions.

A movement in the sky, a flicker of wings crossing the setting moon, caught her eye, and she stood straighter. "Kamin, I see something odd, there in the sky, just below the constellation of Osiris."

"What?" He raised his head from his contemplation of the map, obliterated her painstakingly drawn representation of the route to the enemy's fortress with one sweeping gesture of his large hand and came to join her. Peering in the direction she pointed, he said, "It's a bird."

"Some kind of owl?" She heard a keening cry, and the bird veered closer, soaring high above them, drifting on a thermal breeze.

Drawing her with him, Kamin headed purposefully toward their stack of gear. "No, it's a falcon."

"They don't fly at night," she protested, suddenly uneasy.

"The Great One Horus reminds us we need to move, find a safe place to rest during the day. It'll be dawn all too soon, and the Hyksos will be out hunting for us." He handed her the nearly depleted water skin before taking the rest of their gear himself.

Nima stumbled. Instantly, he steadied her with one strong hand on her elbow. She asked, "You—you don't think they might give up? I'm nothing but a dancer from a frontier town—"

"And I'm a spy who knows a lot about their most secret plans," Kamin answered grimly. "Although the young officer I killed was the only man in the camp who knew I was anything more than an ordinary prisoner."

"Unless he told Amarkash," Nima said.

"Doesn't matter, either way it's too soon for them to call off the hunt. I wouldn't, if I were in command, not yet." Kamin sounded very sure as he gave his opinion.

"Where are we going to hide?" She scanned the horizon anxiously. "We left the sandstone wadis behind hours ago. No caves here."

"We'll find something."

"Do you have the heiroglyph for confidence in one of your names perhaps?" Nima teased. "You're always so sure the Great Ones will provide an answer to any dilemma."

Kamin grinned but shook his head. "Let's follow the direction the falcon went."

They made considerable progress during the last hours of night, covering a lot of ground. As the sun rose in the east, Kamin eyed the sky to the west of them with severe misgivings. The wind picked up, plucking at their cloaks. "I think we could be in trouble," he said.

"Again?" Nima grabbed at the flapping edges of her cape. Putting the hood over her hair, she sighed. "Sandstorm?"

He pointed at the horizon to the west. "See the band of yellow clouds?"

"I've seen such clouds before, never a good omen. The troupe was in Zauimu once when the storm blew for three days. We couldn't set foot outside the tavern where we were staying. I came to develop a hatred for the place." Eyes wide, she examined their surroundings. "What will we do? If we're caught in the open, the sand will scrub the flesh from our bones."

"There's something over there, way in the distance." He pointed.

"I don't see anything." Squinting, she was dubious. "Could it have been a mirage?"

"I've told you I was gifted by Horus with exceptional vision. Trust me." He started jogging, tugging her with him. "I don't care if it's a house, a rock outcropping, some trees, at this point we need shelter."

A falcon screamed in the sky, winging ahead of them, skimming the ground. The wind blew harder, and small dust devils swirled on all sides of them as they reached the rocks Kamin had seen. Again, the falcon issued a warning or a challenge, swooping at Kamin.

Nima stared at the barren rock formation. "Not too promising, is it? What are we going to do now?"

The falcon made another pass, winging low over the ground to the left, uttering low-voiced cries. With narrowed eyes, Kamin watched the bird's trajectory. "I say we follow the bird."

Nima nodded. "For lack of a better plan, I agree, and we need to move fast."

They broke into a run. Nima ordered herself to move, fighting exhaustion. Kamin ran easily, not even breathing hard. As if checking on them, the bird made lazy circles in the ever-more-ominous sky. Behind the façade of the rocks, the terrain sloped, and Nima found herself in a valley with tumbledown stone ruins in a heap at the far end. Plummeting out of the sky with heart-stopping speed, the falcon shrieked, landing atop the tallest ruin, watching as they came closer.

"Here? Where's the safe shelter here?" Nima asked, hands on her hips, her skeptical glance switching from one piece of broken masonry to the next. The muscles in her legs quivered and ached, so she sank onto a convenient pillar remnant, rubbing her calves. "There isn't even an intact building."

"Most likely this was a small temple in ancient times, maybe even the first civilization before ours." Kamin walked closer to the broken columns, half buried in the sand. Sidling along the jagged edge of the roof, the falcon tilted its head to watch. "Come see this."

"What did you find?" Wearily, Nima got up from her seat on a column base and trudged to join him.

"Maybe this was the center of the temple." Kamin kicked at the sand and dry brush drifted across the flat space. More of the painting became visible—gazelles running through a forest growing beside a body of water. Flowers bloomed in vast carpets of sadly faded color, and the trees were laden with fruit. The hues were faint now but must have been vivid eons ago.

"Not in the modern style but beautiful." Nima walked over to examine the flowers more closely.

The falcon winged past her, landing at the far edge of the patio, pecking at one particular flagstone with its beak before taking off again. Moving to the place indicated by the falcon, Kamin hunkered to examine the exposed floor closely. A gust of wind blew stinging sand, and they both had to stand, clutching each other for stability, backs to the gale. As soon as the wind eased, Kamin returned to the stone, rapping his knuckles on it in various spots. Running the tips of his fingers along the seam between the stone and its neighbors, he tried to pry the block up. Drawing his dagger, he used the blade as a lever. "I think this might be a trapdoor. Ah, got it."

Moving out of the way as the painted slab he'd been working on slid aside, Kamin watched as it shifted in fits and starts under the stone next to it until a black opening loomed. He leaned over, his head inches above the ground. "Air smells fresh. Fragrant, actually."

Nima didn't trust the trapdoor to be anything resembling good fortune, falcon or no falcon. "Be careful, there could be snakes or scorpions."

"I'll protect you from those plagues, as long as you protect me from spiders. Fair's fair." Grinning, he held out one hand to her. "This must lead somewhere we can shelter from the storm or the falcon wouldn't have led us to it."

"You have a lot more confidence in birds than I do, soldier."

Shrieking around the edges of the rock formation and the ruins, the wind was picking up.

"Horus is the Great One I serve. I can't imagine his falcon would betray us." Taking her hand, he squeezed it gently. "I'll go and let you know how it is in a minute." Stepping into the stairway, Kamin descended. Reluctantly, Nima leaned over the rim, trying to make out any features in the inky black depths, straining to hear the sound of his footsteps as they receded, growing fainter.

"Can you see anything?" she called after a few moments when she heard him walking toward her in the tunnel below.

"The passage opens into a lighted area. I didn't go all the way to the end." Kamin emerged partway from the tunnel, resting his arms on the ground, regarding her with a frown. "I think we'd better hide here because we're out of time to look for a better shelter from this weather. Trust me, trust Horus. All right?"

Taking a deep breath, one hand over her stomach to quell the nervous flutters, she let him draw her over the edge of the opening, then descended the steps by feel, going deeper into the near-total darkness.

Reaching the bottom with an awkward thump, expecting there to be more stairs, Nima peered into the gloom, eyes narrowed. She was ready for anything, pulse pounding, fight or flight. As he'd promised, light beckoned at the end of the inky blackness. The air was fresh, carrying the scent of some lush flower. *Lotus here? So far from the Nile?*

"What are you doing?" she asked, squinting at Kamin as he circled her to ascend the staircase.

"Trying to get the trapdoor closed," he grunted. There was a loud snap, and she heard the panel sliding home. Kamin descended the stairs in a rush.

Hand over her heart as it thumped loudly in her chest, Nima squinted in his direction. "Can you get the capstone to open again when we're ready to leave?"

"Probably." His teeth flashed white in that cocky grin as he dusted his hands off. "There was a latch." Taking her by the elbow, he led her forward in the narrow tunnel.

After about thirty paces, they stood on the threshold of the portal, mere steps away from a lush garden. Palm trees and other greenery grew at the edges of an azure lake. Birds of all colors flew in the sky or rested in the tree branches. Gazelles like the ones in the ancient temple painting ambled past. A riot of pastel-hued flowers bloomed in clumps scattered over a carpet of lush, green grass.

"How can this be? How can such things exist under the ground?" Hand over her mouth, goose bumps prickling her skin, Nima shrank against Kamin's reassuringly solid frame. "What is this place? Are we dead? Is this the Afterlife?"

"We're not dead," he said. "We didn't pass through any chamber of judgment, did we?"

"No. But this place is too perfect to be real." On tiptoe, as if stepping into the edge of the Nile, Nima advanced onto the grass, finding the surface thicker under her aching feet than the best carpet. Pirouetting to Kamin, she extended one arm to him. "Pinch me."

He recoiled. "*What*?"

"Pinch me, I want to be sure I'm not dreaming."

Chuckling, he obliged, a little nip at her forearm above the bead amulet. "So, are you awake?"

Rubbing the spot in greatly exaggerated chagrin, she nodded.

A fawn walked up to her, nuzzling her skirts. Delighted, she reached out to pet the baby animal's soft brown and white-spotted flanks. After sniffing Kamin's pack, the creature bounded off in awkward leaps a moment later, hastening to its mother, grazing a few yards away.

"This could be *part* of the Afterlife, though," Kamin said, staring after the fawn. "No wild animal should be so comfortable in the presence of humans."

*****

"Part of the Afterlife?" Nima paused in the act of removing her other sandal, wriggling her toes on the cool grass under her bare feet. "What do you mean?"

Kamin regarded the grassy hillock behind him where the tunnel had been carved to the outer world. "There are rumors—recent tales, not old scribes' legends—claiming some of Pharaoh's closest companions were able to journey through the Afterlife on a quest and return, by the grace of the Great Ones."

Her eyes widened, and her mouth formed a perfect O shape. "Why would anyone seek to travel through the Afterlife before their appointed time?"

"The details aren't known to me." He shrugged. "Someone desperate, no doubt. But perhaps Horus's falcon brought us to…a side door of the Afterlife."

Nima gazed longingly at the lake. "Can we set up camp over there?" Blushing, she looked at her travel-stained dress, hands spread wide. "I crave a bath."

He shifted the packs on his shoulders. "Why not? One place is as good as any. Although, I don't want to get too far away from this door. The lake may harbor fish, which would be a further blessing."

Beautiful face set in a troubled frown, Nima laid her hand on his arm, as if to hold him in place. "I don't think we should try to harm or kill any living creature here. The mere idea repels me."

"Not even a fish?" Raising his eyebrows, he looked at her in disbelief. "What do we eat then? Flowers? Fruit? I tell you plainly, a soldier travels on his stomach, and mine needs stronger nourishment than stale bread and fruit." He patted his abdomen, loudly rumbling at all this talk of food.

"I'm hungry, too, but my heart holds a strong reluctance. If we're in the Afterlife, shouldn't we pass through and disturb this place as little as possible?" Nima glanced at their beautiful surroundings. "Please, Kamin. We didn't say any blessings. We didn't utter any spells. We ought not to be here probably, so I think we need to tread carefully."

He studied her face. "I admit I couldn't bring myself to kill one of the gazelles right now, much as I crave some meat in my belly. Ordinarily, I don't have qualms about hunting for my dinner, so perhaps you're right."

"Thank you!" Fatigue apparently forgotten, she danced ahead of him, going toward the inviting azure lake in a flurry of twirling dance moves, arms spread.

By the time he arrived at the shore and dropped their gear, she was already unbraiding her hair, battered sandals abandoned on the sandy beach.

"The water's warm," she said. "I dipped a hand in a moment ago. Have you ever seen such white sand?"

Kamin assessed the likelihood of predators lurking in the depths of the lake. *Does paradise harbor Nile crocodiles? Hopefully not.* Judging by how dark blue the water became, the center was deep. A pearlescent haze obscured the horizon. "Stay close to shore and keep a sharp eye out, promise me."

"I don't think we're in any danger here," she said, combing her hair with her fingers. "But as I can't swim, I'll only go a tiny way out into the water." She lifted the hem of her dress and paused, eyeing him.

Obligingly, he did an about-face, seating himself on a handy tree root. "I won't sneak a peek. But I'm not going any farther away than this either, in case you need rescuing."

"Always the warrior. Always on guard." Her voice was light, teasing.

He was glad they'd been able to take shelter in a spot that gave her pleasure, but his instincts told him he'd better remain vigilant no matter how beguiling the surroundings. "A good soldier never abandons the rules of his training. Even in the Afterlife."

He heard her coming across the sand, and then her footsteps whispered over the grass, but he kept himself rigidly facing the forest. Pausing behind him, she bent to drop a kiss on his cheek. A moment later, before he could decide how to react, pattering footsteps told him Nima had danced away toward the lake.

Fabric rustled enticingly as her dress fell to the grass, followed by splashing as she waded into the water. He tried hard to block out the picture of her slender body naked, only a few feet away from him now. *She's traumatized from all she's been through, and she hasn't given any sign of wanting to move beyond mere friendship with me. I told her a little of how I felt, but though she didn't rebuff me, neither did she encourage me.* Nima hummed as she bathed, breaking into song for a bar or two. He heard more splashing and swallowed hard as he visualized her running her hands over all her smooth, soft skin, bathing herself. *I'd have been happy to play lady's maid, touch her beautiful body freely, get us both hot and aroused, before quenching the fire with an unhurried session of lovemaking on this soft grass.*

Eventually, he heard her washing her dress out, sloshing the fabric up and down in the water vigorously.

"Nearly done," she said, a happy lilt in her voice. "Then the lake will be all yours. I'm sorry I've taken so long, but the bath was relaxing."

"No rush. We're here for the rest of the day, perhaps longer, depending on the storm above, which I'll go check on later. I'll get my chance to bathe." Kamin eyed the fruit hanging from the nearby tree. Near to bursting, the luscious plums were full of juice. Maybe in a while he'd climb up and pluck a few, but right now, he wasn't hungry. An apple tree stood beyond the plums, covered in glowing red fruit, but they didn't tempt him either. He frowned momentarily. Hadn't he been ravenous when they walked through the tunnel, impatient to hunt or fish for their dinner?

"All right, you can turn around now," she said, interrupting his thoughts.

He pivoted on the tree root. Nima stood swathed in the Hyksos cloak, having tied it right above her breasts and knotted it at the knees so it wouldn't drag on the ground. The blue dress was neatly spread out on the grass to dry, her undergarments nearby. She shook the glossy curtain of her ebony hair. "Being clean is so luxurious after days as a prisoner and then being on the run. Your turn now."

He stood up, letting his own cloak fall to the ground behind him and kicking off his sandals, and strode to the edge of the water. With relief he unfastened the scratchy Hyksos kilt, tossing the garment aside in a heap. *I wish those barbarians could make civilized clothing.* "The loincloth is next," he warned.

Blushing, Nima moved away, strolling over to the nearest bank of red flowers. "Take your time."

He walked naked into the water, enjoying the sensation as small waves lapped against his body. *I wish we could have shared this.* Reaching the point where the bottom dropped away, Kamin made a shallow dive and came up on his back, floating lazily for a few moments. The sky above was pure blue, no clouds. *Like a painting, not the real sky.* Had the sun moved at all in the time they'd been here? He rolled over and swam rapidly to shore, cutting through the water with his aggressive strokes. *Where's Nima?* He scanned the bank in both directions but didn't see her. Alarmed, he left the water, reaching for his clothing.

As he was fastening the kilt's knotted belt, he called for her. "Nima?"

There was no answer, but he heard singing in the distance, off to the left. Barefoot, he headed rapidly toward the sound. The trees grew more thickly the farther away from the lake he jogged. He met other game animals placidly grazing, none of whom were frightened by his passing, at most raising their heads to watch him stride by. He could hear snatches of a song she was singing, and finally he caught a glimpse of her brown cloak when she walked through a patch of sunlight. Quickening his pace, he caught up to Nima, grabbing her hand.

She stopped humming but swayed to and fro, as if temporarily pausing in a performance. "What's the matter? Did you enjoy the bath?"

"Why did you wander away from the lake?" he demanded, swiveling his head to see how far they'd come. Even with his acute vision, he could barely see the blackness of the tunnel opening in the distance. "What if you'd gotten lost? How would I have found you?"

"It's so beautiful here. I was admiring all the different flowers, and each time I found a new variety, I noticed even more attractive ones farther down the path." She offered him the blossom in her hand, a bloom the size of his fist, the center purple, petals lightening to palest pink at the edges. "This one was by far the most striking."

"Like a jewel," he agreed. "Or a hair ornament." The rich, spicy scent filled his nostrils. *And what was I so worried about?* She'd only been picking flowers. No harm had come to her. Taking the astounding blossom, he placed it in her hair above her ear, then bent to kiss her.

She parted her lips as he ran his tongue lightly over them. He deepened the kiss, molding her body to his, his cock straining the fabric of his loincloth, pressing insistently against her belly. Moaning, she rubbed her pelvis against him. Her breasts under the thin cloak flattened against his bare chest, her nipples hardening in arousal. He brought one hand up to caress her breast. "The velvet petals of the flower can't compare to the softness of your skin," he murmured, lost in a sensual overload, stroking his palm over her budded nipple.

The grass was so thick underfoot, like a mattress. *Why don't I take her cloak off and spread it out for us to lie on? Then we can make love in comfort.* He reached for the knot she'd tied at the top, and she put a hand up to help him untangle the ends of the fabric.

A little alarm bell sounded in his head. *Less than an hour ago, she hadn't even wanted me to watch her bathe. And I'd resolved not to rush her, so what's different now?*

Reluctantly, he ended the kiss to take a breath and slow them down, but Nima tugged at him. Exerting more force, but careful not to bruise her soft skin, he held her at arm's length. She frowned, fingers locked onto his forearms. "Why are you hesitating?" she said, tilting her head.

"Are you sure you want this right now? You want me to make love to you?" *I can't believe I'm asking this, but something's not right.*

She glanced at the surroundings, let go of him and gathered the half-open cloak to cover more of her luminescent skin. "Don't you desire me?"

"More than anything, but--" She moved into his arms and resumed the kiss, grasping his cock through the folds of kilt and loincloth with one hand. He groaned and broke the embrace off again. His soldier's instincts were pricking at him harder and harder, like the point of a knife in the ribs. "Are you hungry?" he asked.

"I was, but I haven't been for a while now." Eyebrows drawing together in a frown, Nima licked her lips. "Why aren't I hungry? Why didn't I pick any fruit? I was going to, but then the flowers caught my eye. Kamin—"

A gazelle butted him in the small of his back. Keeping his hold on Nima, he half turned to find the herd gazing at him with large, expressive brown eyes as they moved into position flanking him.

Yawning, Nima sank bonelessly to her knees, pulling her hand from his clasp as she did so. "I'm tired, and the perfume of these flowers is making me sleepy. Let me rest, then we can make love."

"No, don't sleep." He tugged her to her feet, one of the larger animals pushing its head under her arm to assist him. "We have to get out of here."

This place is not for the likes of you.

The voice rang in his head, but he saw only gazelles. Were *they* talking to him? *Am I losing my mind?*

The quiet voices in his head continued to utter warnings.

Stay too long, and you'll never leave.

Stay too long, and you'll sleep the sleep of eternity.

"Exactly what I'm afraid of," he said out loud. Grimly, he put one arm around Nima's waist and steered her toward the tiny black square in the distance. Forcing her to keep walking with him, Kamin narrowed his focus to the mouth of the tunnel leading to their world. His legs trembled; he felt exhausted for no reason. The short swim hadn't worked his muscles to such a degree. A doe came up beside him, and he curled his free arm around her muscular neck, letting the animal provide him support while he coaxed a barely conscious Nima to remain on her feet. His arms were losing their strength.

Nima slipped from his grasp, falling to the lawn and curling up like a beautiful caterpillar. Rolling his shoulders, Kamin took a deep breath. The gazelles waited. Bending, ignoring the spots of blackness flashing in front of his eyes, he picked her up so he could stagger forward. Two of the animals closed in on either side to keep him upright. Eyes fixed on the promise of the tunnel entrance in the distance, he took one step after another. Exhaustion ate at him. The muscles in his legs burned. He had the overwhelming desire to set Nima on the fragrant grass, spoon himself around her and forget his cares for a few hours. *Why not a quick nap, a refreshing few minutes, then we'll resume our hike?*

The gazelle on his left bumped his body hard, sending a reviving spike of energy through him. Stiffening his stance, Kamin kept moving. His peripheral vision was narrowing, as if he were falling asleep even while walking. Even though Kamin wasn't easily intimidated by mortal foes or danger at any time, the idea of a living death here in the underworld sent fear prickling through his limbs, generating another burst of welcome energy.

"Why would Horus send us here, if it's so deadly?" he asked out loud, hoping the sound of his own voice might help him stay alert.

Words rang in his head, crisp disembodied voices full of concern:

Horus is a god of the sky, not the underworld.

He wished you to be safe from those who hunt you in the outer world.

He may not realize how the soul-sustaining energy here affects the living.

This corner of the Afterlife is not meant for your kind.

"Yeah, I understand we shouldn't be here." Kamin shook his head, trying to shatter the dazed feeling, bit his lip hard enough to taste blood. Spiking through his head, the tiny pain jangled him into action, ordering himself to keep moving. He glanced at Nima, now totally unconscious in his arms, her chest barely rising and falling with shallow breaths. Raising his eyes, he estimated the remaining distance to the portal. Surely it was closer. "If we don't get out of here, the Hyksos win, their evil god wins. And I'm not going to let her die."

There was no answer. The gazelles stayed with him, which was encouraging. Barely conscious now, Kamin trudged forward, stopping for ever-lengthening periods of time, before his four-legged companions nudged him into motion. The tunnel opening loomed larger and larger. He passed the lake. *Grind out a few more steps, last another few moments. Count ten steps then ten more, keep moving.*

He crashed to his knees, Nima sprawling onto the soft grass. Head spinning, Kamin fought to stay conscious. He braced his upper body on his fisted hands, which sank deep into the lush grass and the cool, black earth underneath. Nima rolled over and moaned in her sleep, cloak falling partway open to reveal a tantalizing amount of her lush body. Bending low, he kissed her cheek before rearranging the cloak with clumsy fingers to cover her. One more time he got himself to his feet and lifted her, struggling forward, so tired he moved in zigzags, but generally in the right direction.

One by one the gazelles wandered away, until only two remained, bracing his body like oversized guard dogs. He felt the difference under his bare feet as he stepped onto the hard surface of the tunnel floor. The pressure from the gazelles stopped as the last pair left him, pausing short of the passage out of the underworld. He collapsed, managing to cushion Nima's fall by rolling sideways as his consciousness ebbed away. *I made it to the damn tunnel. Why aren't we reviving?* Unable to do more than breathe, utterly spent, he rolled over, eyes fixed on the cracked stone ceiling. *A few minutes to recuperate then I'll get us up.* He fumbled blindly in the darkness for Nima. Sliding his palm along the smooth skin of her arm until he reached her hand, he linked his fingers with hers and allowed his heavy eyelids to close.

CHAPTER FOUR

Sun glaring through his closed eyelids and the hard surface under his increasingly aching back woke him. *This is the most unforgiving mattress I've ever slept on.* Nima's soft hair spread across his arm, her head pillowed on his shoulder. Opening his eyes, squinting against the sunlight, Kamin grunted and moved her limp body enough to be able to sit up himself. Head spinning, he worked his way from the prone position.

They were outside, in the middle of the painted terrace, their packs lying to the side.

"How in the name of the gods did we get here?" *The last thing I remember is collapsing right inside the tunnel. Maybe one of the gods took pity on us, sent the ushabti to carry us the rest of the way to safety? Since I managed to nearly get us out of there?*

Wind blew gently across the ruins surrounding them on all sides. Realizing how exposed they were should the Hyksos be anywhere in the vicinity, Kamin shook Nima. Finally, he lifted her to a sitting position against him. "Nima, wake up. We've got to move."

Her eyelids fluttered open for a second then drifted shut again. He took the water skin, now replenished, and put it to her lips. "Drink some water. Time to stop dreaming."

She gave a quiet moan of protest but sat up on her own. After her first few sips, her eyes widened, and she turned slowly one way then the other, water forgotten. "Kamin—"

"What do you remember?" Taking the container from her hand, he gulped cool liquid.

"Something about a lake. And deer—no," she corrected herself. "A herd of gazelles. Was it a dream?" She fingered her clean blue dress, though he had no memory of her putting clothes back on.

Reaching out , Kamin plucked the purple and pink flower from her hair, handing it to her. "No dream." He stood up. "I think we were lucky to survive."

Still sniffing the flower's fading perfume, she clasped the hand he stretched out to help her and came to her feet. "You kissed me. I remember now."

"I want to do it again." He pulled her close. She came into his embrace easily, pressing herself to him, raising her face for his kiss. Keeping the caress light, a brief meeting of the lips, he ignored the surge of arousal sweeping through his body. He took her hands and kissed the palms lightly before releasing her and stepping away. "But now is not the time or the place."

She put her arms by her sides. "I can't argue. My spine is tingling. I'm expecting the pain of an arrow striking home any moment." Shivering, she raised her eyes to the rim of the tiny hollow in which the ancient temple lay in ruins. "We'd be easy to capture here."

He was belting his sword on. "Agreed. We need to move out."

"Why is this pack so heavy?" Nima opened the flap, peering at the contents inside. Reaching in, she brought out a plum as big as his fist and showed it to him. "The bag is full of fruit from—from *there*. Do you think we dare eat it?"

Hands on his hips, Kamin blew out his breath then shook his head at the glowing purple fruit. "I don't know. I've been told if you eat anything in the underworld, you won't be able to leave. Water is fine because it flows between here and there, but not food."

"But we have left. You rescued us. We're in our proper place, our world." Nima stamped one foot on the dusty pavement for emphasis. "Surely whoever or whatever loaded this bounty into our pack didn't mean us any harm."

"Horus didn't mean us any harm, but he sent us to shelter in a place where we would've been trapped in eternal sleep. Or worse." Hating to disappoint her, Kamin nonetheless took the pack and set it on the ground. "Even though I'm guessing the servants of the gods must have given us these gifts, I say we leave all of it here, as an offering to the spirits of this old temple. A token of our thanks for sheltering us." He pointed at the blossom in her hand. "That as well."

She did as he requested, laying the flower on top of the leather pack. Within moments, the petals shriveled and faded, decaying as they watched. Nima glanced around the ruins, rubbing her arms as if chilled. "I really want to be away from this place."

"No argument from me," Kamin said. He held out his hand, and as soon as she clasped his fingers, he led her off the frescoed terrace by the shortest route.

Making quick work of the hike to the lip of the bowl-shaped depression, Kamin stopped in his tracks so suddenly Nima bumped into him. "What is it? What's the matter?"

She stepped around him since he made no move to prevent her and came to a sliding halt herself. The sandy soil was crisscrossed with tracks—men, horses, chariot wheels. Kamin walked closer, kneeling to check the imprints. "Hyksos all right. Their wheels are built differently than ours, wider." He stood, dusting his hands. "But these tracks are at least two days old, judging by the condition of the horse dung."

"Two days?" Mouth open, she gaped at the large area the enemy had occupied. "But when we arrived here yesterday, there were no tracks."

Kamin retrieved the pack. "I think we were in that corner of the Afterlife longer than we realized. Horus's plan worked to the extent the Hyksos obviously didn't find us. But now they're somewhere ahead of us on the route to the Nile, and we'll have to be even more careful."

"I wish they didn't want to recapture us so badly," she said as they hiked through the churned-up ground and struck off to the east. "This trip is full of enough perils without those jackals breathing down our necks every moment."

"On the positive side, it shows how important my information must be," Kamin said. "All the more reason we have to make good time and get to the nomarch as soon as we can."

*****

They spent the day sheltered behind a small rock formation at the foot of a great sand dune. It wasn't a secure location, and neither could settle in to rest. By midafternoon they'd mutually agreed remaining was a waste of time, and they marched into the desert, still bearing east.

Hours later, Nima toiled up the rise in front of her and stumbled to a halt, grateful for a sunset breeze brushing the sand. Beside her, Kamin was staring into the shimmering distance, his face set in unhappy lines. Following the direction of his gaze, shielding her eyes with one hand, Nima said, "What is that?"

"A caravan. We've come to one of the major north-south caravan routes."

She turned to him in surprise. "You don't sound pleased. Can't we blend in with them, travel with them?"

"Caravan masters want to be paid for providing transport and safety." He frowned at her. "Not only do we not have anything to buy our passage with, the Hyksos are probably still chasing us and they do have gold to buy friends, informants and allies. Best we wait for this caravan to pass and then go on our way."

"Too late. I think we've been spotted." Nima pointed at the road, where a small group of men on horseback had broken away from the long column, galloping toward them in a cloud of dust.

"Set's teeth, just what we don't need. Stay close and let me do the talking." Drawing his sword, Kamin pulled her closer, shielding her as best he could while the men rode up and encircled them.

"What do we have here?" asked the lead rider, staring at them while his horse tossed its head, chomping on the bit.

"Travelers, like you," Kamin answered neutrally. "We're waiting for your caravan to pass, and then we'll be on our way."

Chewing on a carved sliver of ivory clenched in his remaining teeth, the man studied them, while his companions waited in silence. "You travel lightly." He waved one arm in a broad gesture, tassels on the horse's reins dancing in the breeze. "And the desert is vast."

"We'll be fine, thank you." Kamin kept his eyes locked on the leader. "No need to tarry on our account."

The caravan crew member took the sliver of ivory out of his mouth, picking thoughtfully at his gums for a moment. "What kind of a host would my master be, allowing you to trudge through the sand when you could travel with us in comfort?" The words were kind, but the voice was mocking. "He bid me fetch you."

"We don't travel in the direction you're going." Jaw set, Kamin hefted the sword, raising it in a threatening gesture. "Our road lies to the east."

"Sit by our fire this evening at least." The persistent rider gestured to the road in the distance. "We're making camp now, at the well here."

Nima could tell Kamin was annoyed, as his voice got deeper and his words even more clipped each time he replied to a comment. "We've no gold to pay for the privilege."

"Have I asked for payment?" Making a mock bow over his patient horse's neck, the other man spoke again. "My master insists. A caravan wins favor in our gods' eyes when we help a struggling traveler." The dark eyes stared boldly at Nima. "And his woman."

Kamin put his free arm around Nima's waist. "Exactly. *My* woman." He ignored her surprised, sideways glance. "I tell you again, we've no desire to join your campfire, this night or any other."

"But we are many and you are only one, warrior." The threat was clear. The other riders crowded in more closely, the loose circle becoming the unmistakable jaws of a trap. The man grinned. "Put away your sword and accept our kind invitation."

Grabbed without warning by a pair of stout arms, Nima was torn from Kamin, lifted into the air, landing on the saddle with a thud, and held close to the caravan rider who'd snatched her, the smell of his sweat and musk an unpleasant aroma. She cursed him in Egyptian and several other languages, trying to pry his arm away from her waist as he laughed and wheeled the half-rearing horse in a grand gesture that made her dizzy. The ground was frighteningly far away from a horse's back. Her captor set his steed racing for the caravan road. Hands locked around the raised front of the elaborate saddle, she turned her head once, worried for Kamin. The rider's flying robes blocked her view. The horse's rapid motion across the ground gave her vertigo, so Nima squeezed her eyes shut and prayed to whichever Great Ones might be listening

The caravan was spread out around the large stone wellhead. Men were unloading weary, protesting camels and donkeys. Gaily striped tents were being raised. All manner of people bustled around. The workers stopped their activity, eyeing Nima curiously as she was carried through the chaos to the largest tent. Checking his horse in another showy move, the rider handed her down, where she was enfolded in someone else's grasp the moment her feet touched the ground and hustled into the tent.

"Let me go," she said, jerking her arm free and elbowing her new oppressor sharply in the ribs. "What have you done with my companion?"

"Don't worry, he'll be here in a moment, lovely one," said a deep, melodic voice.

Angry, she turned, raising her line of sight a foot to take in the owner of the sensual voice—a tall man waiting behind her, hands on hips, legs akimbo. Good-looking in a rough-hewn fashion, long black hair tied back with a leather thong, he had ritual scars dotted on both cheeks. Dressed in dusty blue and brown robes and odd leggings tucked into his boots, he wore an elaborate collar of hammered gold beads. An unfamiliar circular emblem in the center matched the scars. Bowing, he thumped one fist over his heart and threw out his other arm expansively. "Caravan Master Ptahnetamun, at your service. And you are?"

"Nima. I didn't ask to be your guest," she said, straightening her dress as best she could.

"No, but I give my hospitality anyway," he answered with a flash of white teeth. "We don't often encounter travelers in this stretch of the desert. You're a blessing from the gods."

"A blessing?" *I don't like the sound of that.* Frowning, Nima took an instinctive step away from the caravan master.

Ptahnetamun bowed his head, grinning even more widely. "Your arrival represents something new to relieve the boredom of our travel."

Said the cat to the mouse. Not much liking the tone of the conversation so far, she racked her brain for some way out of the mousetrap. Hearing horses behind her, Nima turned, relieved to see Kamin jump down from the mount on which he'd been forced to ride double. His sword was missing, which wasn't an encouraging sign about the truth of their situation as guests.

"Of course you'll be in my debt," said their titular host, walking over to a small table and lifting a wineskin. He glanced over his shoulder.

Ignoring the assembled caravan members, shoving his way through the crowd, Kamin strode over to her. "Are you all right?"

Managing a smile, Nima nodded. "I'm fine. This is Ptahnetamun, the caravan master."

Arm around her waist, Kamin ignored the horn cup the man was now holding out to him. "All we want is to continue on our way."

"Spoken like one accustomed to command," Ptahnetamun said, raising his eyebrows as he lifted the cup to drink deep. Wiping his mouth on one flowing sleeve, he handed the cup to a servant girl standing behind his seat. "But I command here."

Leaning slightly into Kamin for reassurance, Nima asked, "What do you want of us?"

"I told you—diversion, amusement." His wide smile returning, the caravan master waved the now refilled cup his servant had just handed him. Half the contents sloshed onto the rugs covering the tent floor. "Profit perhaps." He drank what remained in one gulp.

"We don't wish to travel north, and we've no gold to pay for provisions or shelter. You'll realize no profit from us," Kamin said.

Ptahnetamun eyed him for a minute. "By the look of you, you're fugitives. Escaped slaves maybe?" He waited, but neither Kamin nor Nima spoke. Idly scratching at one of his facial scars, he turned to the man who'd led the group that took them prisoner. "There might be profit in having these two as my—guests, eh? Whoever is looking for them might appreciate our help." Rubbing two fingers together in the universal sign for coin, he guffawed, the rest of the audience in the tent joining in raucous laughter.

He knows something about us. Maybe the Hyksos have put out word they're searching for us. Realizing Kamin's abilities as a fighter weren't going to save them this time, a sketchy idea taking shape in her mind, Nima took a deep breath to soothe her nerves. "You can't have it both ways, sir," she said when the laughter quieted, laying one hand on Kamin's arm as a calming gesture. *Please, Great Ones, let him follow my lead now.* "Either we're going to be your guests or your prisoners."

"Good point." Ptahnetamun poured himself another round of the wine before sitting down. "It seems we're on the horns of a dilemma."

He likes toying with us. Hoping she'd found a way out of the situation, Nima took a chance. "Are you a gambling man?" She pointed at the object taking up most of the table beside him. "Do I see a senet board?"

He rubbed his hand across the game board inlaid atop the gleaming container. "Indeed it is. You play?"

As if she had all the time in the world, Nima walked to the game box, deliberately making her stride slow and sensuous, like the opening steps of a dance. Bending to give him a good view of her shapely bottom outlined by the dress pulled tight as she leaned over, Nima opened the bottom drawer of the case and plucked a shiny black pawn at random from inside. With an elegant gesture, she turned and extended her hand to the caravan master, the pawn sitting on her flat palm. "I challenge you to a game."

He stroked his bearded chin, leaned back as he braced one foot on a trunk and made a show of considering. "For what stakes?"

"If I win, you give us shelter for the night, and we go our separate ways in the morning." She set the pawn on the board in the starting square. "If you win, we're yours to do with as you please."

"Nima—" Kamin's protest was instant and angry. In two steps he was at her side, yanking her to face him. "What are you—"

Wrenching herself loose, she ignored him, facing Ptahnetamun again. "I've lived in border towns all my life, so I've heard of the honor code governing caravan masters. I want your word you'll abide by the outcome of the game." She held up one hand before he could speak. "No, I want your blood oath on it."

Jaw dropping, Ptahnetamun stared at her while his men muttered and even the serving girl looked impressed by Nima's boldness.

"Well? Do you agree to my terms or don't you?" Nima drew herself to her full height and tried to feel impressive, despite her dusty clothes and tired body. *He can't back down from this challenge in front of his crew. I hope.* Since he hesitated, she taunted him, paraphrasing a saying she'd often heard in the taverns where she danced. "Be aware I'll pass you by as one who sails with the breeze, blessed by the Sun. I'll be entering the House of Repeating Life while you, my opponent, *will* be stopped."

Next minute, Ptahnetamun threw back his head, roaring with laughter. "Spoken like a true gambler. I like your spirit, woman." He pointed at Kamin. "Does your warrior agree to what you propose? The deal must include you both."

"Will you give us a moment?" Pulling Kamin aside, Nima turned so the gawking caravan crew couldn't see their faces. Kamin's cheeks were red, and his frown was truly impressive.

Putting both hands on her shoulders, he gave her a little shake. "What in the seven hells are you doing?"

She laid her hand gently over his mouth, leaning close as she whispered, "Trust me, please, Kamin? If he swears me a blood oath—"

Shoving her hand away, he rolled his eyes. "And *if* you win," he said furiously. "The throwing sticks are bound to be false-weighted somehow. It won't be a fair game, not some friendly match in the tavern for mugs of beer."

"I'm hoping the sticks *are* false." She smiled mischievously, letting her smile fade as he continued to glare at her. "Please? I know the stakes are high, but we're not getting out of here otherwise. You're one man surrounded by dozens, and he sees profit in selling us. This is the only way we stand a chance of escaping."

"You're asking me to risk the success of my mission for Pharaoh, for *Egypt*, on how well you can cheat a cheater?" He closed his eyes for a moment, rubbing his brow.

"Blood oath?" Ptahnetamun asked from his position next to the game board.

Going on tiptoe to look over Kamin's shoulder, Nima said magnanimously, "Nothing less. I'll swear as well," drawing a quickly smothered laugh from the ever-increasing crowd at her back.

"She's set the stakes." The man who'd taken Nima on his horse came forward to offer the caravan master his dagger. "Challenge has been made."

"And accepted!" Ptahnetamun slammed his cup on the table so forcefully the base cracked. Rolling back his sleeve, he extended his thick wrist. "I swear by the twin gods of the caravan road to abide by the outcome of this senet game. She and her man go free in the morning if she wins." He leered at Nima. "But she'll be on her back in my bed by dawn if I win." The crowd roared with amusement at this sally. Gesturing at Kamin, he finished his boasting. "Be sure I'll sell his carcass for a tidy profit."

Nima said nothing, but laid her wrist across his. After searing the tip of his blade in a candle's flame, the caravan worker nicked each of them in turn with his dagger. Their blood dripped onto the candle, which blazed up in a purple and red explosion of sparks for a second. "Oaths accepted," the man declared.

Ptahnetamun and Nima turned to Kamin.

"My word as a warrior of Pharaoh, I'll accept the outcome." Kamin's oath was given through clenched teeth.

"Done!" Ptahnetamun wrapped a scrap of black cloth around his wrist as Nima pressed hers against her side to stop the blood flow. "We'll play this monumental game later, in the evening after the work of setting up camp and caring for the animals is done. Take these two away until then."

The guards hustled the pair to a small tent close by, shoving them rudely inside. The enclosure was empty, although after a few minutes the serving girl brought a small water skin and a bowl of dried fruit. Having finished efficiently binding the small cut on her wrist with a strip torn from the side seam of her cloak, Nima sank cross-legged on the floor, munching a fig. Kamin paced restlessly. She patted the bare earth next to her. "Come sit, conserve your energy."

He paused for a second, eyeing her with a frown. "I'm strongly tempted to escape right now, while they're preoccupied setting up their camp."

"Leaving me behind?" Nima offered him a fig. "I swore a blood oath, remember? There's no debt between us, soldier. If you think you'll do better on your own, then don't fret over me. For your information, I do intend to win the game, gods willing."

"I gave my word too." He took the fruit, chewing slowly. "Of course I wouldn't abandon you. But to have everything balancing on a game of senet—"

"What is life itself but a game of senet?" she said philosophically. "He wasn't going to let us go. I think he knows we're worth something to the enemy, so I took the only chance I saw."

"He should abide by his blood oath," Kamin agreed. "If you win." He brought her the water and sat, pulling Nima to lean against him. "You did maneuver him quite cleverly, I'll grant you that."

She grinned, taking another fig. "Now if I can do the same on the senet board."

*****

After sunset, the guards escorted Nima and Kamin to the main campfire, around which the majority of the caravan crew and paying passengers had gathered. Ptahnetamun sat on a blue and gold-striped cushion atop a lion-footed stool in the center of the crowd, with the senet board open on a low table in front of him. Rising at their approach, he gestured to the matching stool across from him. "Will you be seated, Lady Nima?"

As she sank onto the slightly padded seat, the servant girl came forward from the rear of the tent, carrying a wine decanter and mugs on a wooden tray. With a flourish, their host poured. "I've broken out some of the finest wine from my cargo, the special stock rated as three-times-good, in honor of our high-stakes wager. What the tax collectors don't know, won't trouble them. Can't tax what doesn't exist, eh?" With a wink, he handed her a mug brimming with wine. "A toast, to our mutual enjoyment of the game."

Nima tapped his mug with hers and drank deeply. Kamin took a place behind her, wishing for the thousandth time that he could have devised another way out of this situation for them both. *I hope she realizes he's trying to get her drunk, no matter how prized a vintage this wine may be.* His heart sank as he remembered her stating on the first night of freedom that she'd no head for wine.

"We'll throw to see who goes first," Ptahnetamun announced. "Each white side showing counts as one point."

"Plus, the extra point if all four sides come up white." Nima nodded, taking one of the four painted throwing sticks in her hand, turning it as if admiring the intricate floral paintings enameled on the glossy black side. Kamin hoped she was actually gauging the weight. Gathering the other three sticks now, rubbing them together against her palms a few times, she cast them on the table.

Three black sides, one white. Kamin heard furious wagering going on in the crowd around them, steep odds against Nima winning. Hardly encouraging.

Ptahnetamun cast three white sides, one black, winning the honor of going first since he'd scored three points to her one. Selecting the taller black pawns, he set them on the first five squares.

Kamin looked at the board, stark obsidian and iridescent mother of pearl set into ebony wood, the colors alternating, gleaming in the firelight. Hieroglyphics and symbols had been etched in gold on certain especially significant squares. Thirty squares in three long rows, five pawns for each player. Had his life ever rested on such a flimsy hope? At least in battle he was master of his own fate, wielding sword and shield, his brother soldiers to each side. Here he was relying, yet again, on Nima—a dancer, not a warrior. *Why did I allow myself to be placed in this position, like one of the pawns in front of me?*

Someone passed him a mug of wine, and he drank deeply, carelessly. *Because no matter what I said an hour ago in the tent, I'd never leave her.* He owed her for rescuing him from the Hyksos camp. Additionally, this brave, smart woman was gaining an ever-growing space in his heart. His brother warriors would laugh themselves sick at the idea of him falling for a dancer. Glancing at the sky, Kamin saw a highly unseasonal flash of lightning skipping through the clouds in the distance. Thunder rumbled as Ptahnetamun made his first throw, advancing one pawn onto the fifteenth square. Marked with a golden ankh, this was the gateway to the game.

Kamin sent Horus a silent prayer to watch over Nima, although in truth his patron wasn't known to be intimately involved with senet. Or women. Spilling a bit of the wine as a sacrifice, he hoped Nuit, goddess of the night sky, might find herself intrigued by the game and favor Nima as a fellow female. *Or maybe Renenutet, given the amulet Nima wears. The Snake Goddess is said to have a taste for fine wine.*

This had to be an ancient board, looted from some tomb of the earliest pharaohs perhaps. There was a half-obliterated cartouche on the side closest to him. Who knew how Ptahnetamun had come into possession of such a treasure? Fit for a pharaoh, this set. Maybe the board and pawns carried magic along with the weight of the ages. Perhaps his prayers would do some good. *I certainly can't help Nima in any other way right now.*

Nima threw all black sides, forfeiting the turn. Grinning, her opponent swept the painted sticks up and blew gently on them. "This may be a short game, lady. Perhaps I should send the serving girls to prepare my bed for us now."

"We're a long way from reaching the final five squares, either of us," Nima answered, her face calm, unconcerned. Raising one eyebrow, she sipped at her wine. "Are you going to throw sticks or talk?"

For answer he tossed the counters on the table, coming up all white sides, garnering five points total. Pondering strategy for a moment, he advanced the first pawn off the ankh, moving three spaces with it before shifting his second pawn to the gateway space. Nima threw the same score and got her first pawn onto the board, sharing the ankh space with Ptahnetamun's as the rules allowed, using up two points. Rapidly, she tapped her white, round pawn across the next three spaces, however, sending his second pawn back into limbo as she arrived on the same square.

Frowning, the caravan master made quick work of his toss, two black, two white sides, banishing her single gleaming mother-of-pearl pawn to the staging area of the board again.

Nima got all white on the next throw, earning an extra point. She put two pawns on the main portion of the board, saying as she did so, "Did you know these game pieces are sometimes known as dancers? And as I am a dancer by trade, good luck for me."

"Now you tell me," Ptahnetamun grunted, contemplating his next move. Clearly, he wasn't as yet impressed with her as an opponent.

They battled on, each finally getting all their pawns onto the board but then advancing, falling back, regaining ground or suffering a loss as dictated by the throw of the sticks. As closely as he was watching, Kamin couldn't decide whether the sticks were cheats or not. Certainly the white sides seemed to be falling to Nima's advantage now as often as Ptahnetamun's, much to the latter's displeasure. Nima kept up a light chatter, sipped her wine, seeming unfazed by any temporary setback. She was first to send one pawn all the way through, even past the last five special squares, throwing a two as needed to get her marker out of the House of Re, square number twenty-nine, and safely into the Afterlife. Swearing loudly at her small victory, the caravan master managed to capture her fifth pawn with a victorious roar, sending the game piece back to square fifteen, the House of Rebirth. There the iridescent pawn sat in lonely splendor, obscuring the golden ankh symbol. Doomed to restart its journey through the phases of the game, the white piece seemed to offer no threat to any of Ptahnetamun's pieces.

Kamin felt a cold wind blow over him as Ptahnetamun advanced his next three pawns unscathed off the board, while Nima experienced a crushing lack of high-scoring throws. Kamin knew the man was cheating, had seen him miscount at least twice, but he'd seen Nima do the same, even more skillfully. Since neither game player was calling the other out on their misdeeds, Kamin kept his silence. There was muttering in the crowd, but it seemed the audience admired both the gaming *and* the cheating skills on display and was content to accept the outcome. The betting odds evened out, although still slightly favoring the caravan master to win.

Thunder rumbled as Ptahnetamun marched his fourth pawn off the board. His fifth was ten squares back, and Nima passed him by. There was an audible gasp from the crowd as she threw four white sides, sending her next-to-last pawn to safety. Now the game sat with one pawn belonging to each player still on the board. The wily caravan master was a few squares closer to claiming victory, but Nima was gaining on him, until finally both pawns sat crowded on square twenty-six, the House of Happiness, one of the few spaces that could be so shared.

"Yet only one of us will have happiness within their grasp this night," Ptahnetamun said.

"It's been a good game, well fought," Nima answered, rubbing her thumb along the smooth edges of the sticks in her hand.

She needs four white sides showing to gain the extra point and get off the board. Doubtful she can throw the same score again. He might challenge her amazing luck openly if she did. Kamin didn't know what outcome to hope for. The tension was palpable.

Nima threw two white sides, advancing her pawn to sit alone on square twenty-eight. A score of three would be required next time if she was to win.

Now to pray he can't manipulate the sticks to throw the four white sides and gain the extra point either. Kamin watched intently in the firelight as Ptahnetamun held the sticks an extra second before tossing them with an odd flick of the wrist. As lightning flashed directly overhead and thunder boomed, the markers rolled across the table, fetching up against the side of the board, one tilting from the impact, balancing impossibly on the thin edge for a heartbeat before toppling to conceal its white side at the last second. Frowning, clearly unhappy with his points, their suddenly sober host moved his pawn past Nima's onto square twenty-nine. He would need exactly two points to win the game on his next throw.

Nima collected the wooden sticks one at a time, cupping them in her hands for a long moment. Kamin rested his hand on her shoulder and gave a gentle squeeze. *Surely the gods won't desert her now.* Flashing him a tired smile, Nima dropped the sticks on the table, much as Ptahnetamun had done a few moments before. As the counters rolled and spun, all eyes following their path across the table, a cold breeze swept across the campsite, causing the fire to dance and flicker eerily. One black side, then one white side to secure half the needed points. Two sticks kept going, tumbling ever more slowly. A white side—one more hard-won point. The fourth stick slid lazily across the table, black side showing, before taking an odd jump, ending on the white side and giving her the needed third point.

"You won," Kamin said, half in disbelief.

Deliberately, touching each square in turn, Nima moved her pawn off the board. "Victory is ours."

CHAPTER FIVE

For a long moment, Ptahnetamun said nothing. The crowd held its breath. Kamin tensed, ready to grab Nima by the hand to run into the dark desert as a last effort to gain their freedom, should the man renege on his oath now.

Deliberately, the caravan master tipped his remaining pawn on its side before holding his hand out to Nima. "Congratulations, my lady. Clearly the gods were with you on your final throw. Life, prosperity, health to you."

She shook his hand. "You honor our agreement, then?"

He nodded. "Although it will cost me a great deal of gold." His gaze flicked to Kamin and back to Nima. "There are those hunting you who've offered a staggering price. But the judgment of the gods was clear, and I'll not risk their wrath by breaking my oath." Releasing her hand, Ptahnetamun stood up, throwing his arms wide, stepping into the center of the gathering. "Now we feast to celebrate a hard-fought game!"

Released from tense waiting, the crowd settled the wagers before streaming to where long rugs had been set up for the feast. Women began placing huge platters of food on the low tables.

"Come, be my guests at dinner," Ptahnetamun invited. "I've ordered a goat slaughtered tonight for the occasion, although I will admit I expected to be celebrating my victory, not yours."

Kamin and Nima sat next to him on an elevated platform of tasseled pillows and rugs and sampled the finest food the caravan had to offer. Seeming to bear no grudge, Ptahnetamun regaled them with stories of his wanderings in foreign lands, buying and selling all manner of goods and oddities, and conveying passengers.

"I've a suggestion for you," he said at length. "Travel with me for the next few days."

"We don't journey to the north," Kamin answered, dipping a crust of bread into the spiced yogurt.

"I know, you've been most insistent about going east, to reach your beloved Nile, but sometimes the best route is not actually the most direct." Ptahnetamun leaned forward. "If you keep going east in a straight line from here, there's no oasis to be found, nowhere to get food and water. I doubt your lady dancer can survive such a trek, no offense to her. If you travel with me, around noon of the third day, gods willing, we'll cross a narrow track leading east. Used by herders or smugglers perhaps, not big enough for a caravan, but there are small wells and an oasis or two along the way. I'll give you robes suited to desert travel and enough water to make it to the first resupply point."

Kamin eyed his host, suspicion foremost in his thoughts. "I told you we've no gold or deben to pay, not even for two days of caravan passage."

Ptahnetamun clapped him on the shoulder. "It would be a sin against the gods for me to leave you in the desert, walking to your death, since I've sworn a blood oath to Lady Nima. You look sturdy enough to load and unload camels, work your passage for two days. The lady and I can play—"

"No more senet for high stakes," Kamin said, holding his hand up to stop the flow of words. "She's won her game."

"We could play hounds and jackals perhaps," Nima said from the other side, grinning. "For low stakes."

"I know how to deal with camels." Kamin scooped up his mug of beer and drank.

Realizing Nima was looking askance at him, he set the jug on the table and nodded. "I've done many an odd task in my time. You'd be surprised."

"It's settled then." The caravan master selected a large shank of meat, carving slices with gusto. "Report to my loadmaster in the morning, and he'll assign you to a job."

Nima leaned closer to Kamin, whispering in his ear, "Are you sure?"

Handing her another date, he said, "The man makes sense, as far as the supply of water. Horus might or might not continue to guide us. Besides, the Hyksos wouldn't expect us to head north out of our way, so all in all it's a sound strategy." *Which doesn't mean I have to like it.*

After several courses had been served, a three-man band with drums and flutes set up off to the side and a troupe of dancers came somersaulting into the large clear area in front of their makeshift dais.

Leaning over, Ptahnetamun pointed at the dancers with the wineskin before refilling Nima's cup. "They travel with me and give shows whenever we camp near a town or city. They make a great deal of gold for themselves and for me—you'll enjoy this, something unusual. I asked their troupe master to give a small performance for you tonight."

Men and women were dancing and cavorting together, which was an oddity in and of itself. Strange though he found the dance, Kamin had to admire the skill on display. The performers were obviously not Egyptian, wearing unusually patterned kilts and tunics, their curly black hair tied back with bright-colored ribands. "Where are they from?"

"The land of Minos, across the seas," their host said.

Not taking her eyes from the performance, Nima asked, "Why did they leave their home?"

Ptahnetamun shook his head. "I ask no questions. Anyone who can pay my price is free to travel in my caravan."

The dancing continued, the drumbeat throbbing, the tune unfamiliar but catchy. Kamin could tell Nima was entranced, studying the new moves, swaying in time to the music. Finally, she could stand it no more, rose and stepped from the dais, kilting her skirts high on her hips before skipping in to join the troop.

There was scarcely a ripple in the movement as the Minoans absorbed her into their ranks and began showing off their moves, waiting for her to demonstrate something of her own artistry and then finally all whirling together, with her at the center as the featured performer.

Kamin was enthralled by Nima's performance, as he'd been in the Hyksos camp. She was powerful, confident, beautiful in her joy. Pushing their dance to new heights, the Minoans seemed challenged by her unique artistry in matching movement to music. The foreign dancing was more athletic than sensual, but he couldn't take his eyes off Nima.

Ptahnetamun leaned over. "I would wish she wasn't such an accomplished senet player." He nodded toward the dancers. "She's quite something, your lady."

The dance ended to a deafening round of applause and cheers from the crowd. Flushed, laughing, Nima parted from the others, leaving them to scoop up the few coins thrown by the crowd, and rejoined Kamin.

The caravan master handed her a mug of beer as she fanned herself and readjusted her skirts. "You're better than any of them. You should sign a contract with me and follow my road—I could make you rich and famous, lady, believe it, the way you dance."

"What do you mean?" Nima studied him over the rim of the mug. "I'll be no man's slave."

Ptahnetamun shook his head. "No, no, you mistake me. I've a contract with Andrios, the leader of the Minoan dance troupe, drawn up all proper by one of the god Thoth's temple scribes, witnessed by an Egyptian official in Luxor. The dance troupe pays me a percentage of their earnings in exchange for security and passage along the caravan road. I'd surely offer you the same. We've a blood oath between us, you and I, witnessed by all my men, remember?"

Nima shook her head. "Fine for the Minoans, they're foreigners. I'm Egyptian—I couldn't leave the Black Lands."

"I travel in and out of Egypt all the time. You could dance abroad for a few years, save your gold and then retire anywhere you chose, in Egypt, Thebes even."

Ptahnetamun nudged her in the ribs. "See the world. Live as a lady of luxury, build a tomb as grand as the queen's for a good Afterlife, eh?"

He's just offered her one of her life's dreams on a platter. I wonder if he hopes by keeping us in his company for two more days, he can persuade Nima to join the troupe? Kamin's heart sank. Hating himself but reacting with a jealous instinct he didn't fully understand, angered by the idea of Nima choosing a different road than the one he traveled, he leaned across her to address their host in disparaging tones. "You forget, we're hunted by the Hyksos."

Ptahnetamun scoffed. "I could protect her from them. We don't survive by merely our wits, soldier, not with the treasures and trade goods we carry. My men are tough, well trained. Anyone who attacks us risks the fury of the entire caravan guild. No, even the most determined enemy of Egypt doesn't want to stir up that hornets' nest. They need traders, too. I'm bound out of Egypt right now. By the time we return, they'll have forgotten her. Maybe they'll catch you in the meantime, eh?"

"Despite the way we arrived as your guests, I'm not normally easy to snare," Kamin said, spearing a tender morsel of meat for Nima and putting it on her plate.

Although she thanked him in a low murmur, Nima seemed distracted, thoughtful for the rest of the meal, saying little. When the banquet drew to an end, people drifting away to seek their sleeping mats, she turned to Kamin. "I'm going to visit the dancers for a while, so don't wait up for me. They promised to show me some of those complicated throws and lifts they were doing. Their leader said in Minos, as part of the sacred dance, they vault over the horns of bulls and somersault from the beast's back! Can you imagine? I'd like to see such a performance."

Staring into her face, he wished he could read her mind. How tempted was she by the caravan master's offer? *And why am I so unreasonably upset? Won't it be easier for me to reach my goal faster if I travel alone?* But the idea of journeying anywhere without Nima by his side was suddenly unthinkable.

"She'll be safe anywhere in the camp, soldier," Ptahnetamun said, misunderstanding the concern that must be showing on Kamin's face. "I'll escort her to the dancers' tent myself."

Smiling at Kamin, Nima put one hand on his arm for a moment. "Don't worry."

The pain wrapping itself around his heart as he thought of losing her from his life, made him angry. "It's no matter to me. Do as you please." Turning on his heel, he strode off to the tent they'd been given, fighting the urge with every step to go seek her out. *Until my mission for Pharaoh is done, I can't offer her anything. I'm not free to speak of possibilities.*

*****

Well aware Nima hadn't returned to the small tent they were sharing, Kamin slept fitfully. In the predawn, as he heard the bustle of the caravan packing up to move on, he rose. Wrapping his cloak tightly to keep out the early-morning chill, he strolled outside. His sword and belt knife were stacked beside the tent, and with vast relief he re-armed himself. The serving girl bustled up to hand him a water skin and a pouch.

"Some journey bread, sir, and dried meat, from the master."

He caught her wrist as she moved away to her next task. "Have you seen Nima?"

"No, sir, not since her wonderful dance last night." Making a little sideways movement, awkwardly mimicking a dance step, she sighed. "I wish I could prance like that. I could have any man in the camp then, maybe even the master." Giggling, eyes wide at the mere idea of bedding Ptahnetamun, she hastened away.

Behind him, men were already taking apart the tent he'd slept in, loading it onto a protesting donkey. Not hungry, Kamin slung the small sack of provisions over his shoulder and stalked through the controlled chaos, looking for the loadmaster. Once he'd found the right person, he was rapidly assigned to a team loading camels. The cargo was concealed in bulging sacks and baskets, and Kamin knew better than to ask too many questions about what Ptahnetamun was transporting. Spices, gold, salt, other exotic goods, perhaps.

I'm not one of Pharaoh's tax collectors after all. Slapping the camel standing in his way on the rump, Kamin moved on to help with the next.

The camels were balky as such creatures invariably are. Kamin and the man he was assigned to help had a string of ten camels to load, and the task took more time than either of them wanted. The last camel howled, spat and generally complained, while they adjusted the alignment of the wooden poles bearing the load until the arrangement suddenly met with her satisfaction, and she lumbered to her feet, ready to march.

None too soon, as the caravan workers set up a terrible din banging on pans and bells, the half-mile-long string of camels lurched into motion, one string of animals at a time. Munching a date, Kamin walked along the procession, searching for Nima and the dancers. He found them a few camel strings back from where he'd begun in his assigned spot at the head of the caravan. A group of the women, including Nima, was walking, chatting as they munched on journey bread. Her smile when she saw him warmed his heart. "Did you sleep well then?" he asked, nodding a greeting to the Minoan dancers.

"We stayed up all night, talking," she answered. "Meet Thala and Mika—they've had the most amazing adventures on their travels—"

Has meeting these other dancers stolen her common sense? "You should be resting, preserving your strength." Gesturing at the camel string they were walking beside, knowing he was probably glowering at her, he said, "You should perch on one of the camels, like others have already done, let the animal walk for you."

"Oh, the troupe has a special cart, drawn by donkeys, where we'll ride most of the day," said one of the dancers with Nima, pointing at the vehicle for emphasis.

"Just stretching our legs for now," said the other, toying with her gold hoop earring. She exchanged a knowing glance with the first girl, linked arms and drew her away, leaving Kamin and Nima in some privacy.

They walked in silence for a few moments beside the camels.

"It's just I've never met any truly professional performers, besides the shabby little troupe who raised me," Nima said defensively.

"You owe me no explanations."

He knew she was glancing at him with her eyebrows raised in puzzlement, surprised by his gruffness. How could he explain to her his fear that she'd decide to stay with these exotic people who offered her so much? He could offer as much of a future, or even more perhaps, but not until his mission for Pharaoh was complete. And, truth be told, he was still adjusting to the fact that he could no longer envision a future for himself that didn't include this woman as his partner.

"And you slept well?" Oblivious to his inner turmoil, a moment later, she tried a neutral topic.

Next, we'll be speaking of the unchanging weather no doubt. Kamin grimaced, upset with himself. *I'm not used to constraint between us. I'd better leave her alone before I say something clumsy I'll regret.* "Well enough. I should be getting back, since I'm working our passage." Unable to resist touching her, he put his hand on her arm, enjoying the softness of her skin. "Promise me you'll ride in the cart for as many hours today as you can."

She rewarded him with a smile and a nod.

"I'll see you this evening then, when the caravan camps for the night." Lengthening his stride, he headed to his assigned string of camels, further to the front of the caravan. *What is it about this woman that has my heart tied up in the knots of Isis? She's beautiful and sexy and dances like the goddess Hathor herself, but I've met dancers before and certainly never been tempted to marry one!* Shoving a complaining camel back in line so he could pass, he scanned the countryside they were trekking through. Bare desert as far as the eye could see, broken by a few rocky outcrops. He couldn't fault Ptahnetamun's logic—the two of them were better off with the caravan than on their own in this inhospitable area. Finding water would have been a desperate issue.

He thought back to the first moment he'd laid eyes on Nima, when she'd brought him her cup of water in the Hyksos camp. *Brave, determined to do what's right no matter the cost to her—this woman embodies everything a man could ask for.* Oh, yes, he was head over heels for her and left hoping she might feel the same for him. *And what would my mother and sisters think, when I bring Nima to the door of our family home?* Well, he didn't give a damn what they'd think, but he'd insist they respect her as he did, if necessary. *Truth to tell, my mother would be happy I was settling down, no matter who the woman was. Give her a grandchild, and all would be well in her world.* He grinned.

"Hey, about time you came back," his co-worker greeted him, gesturing impatiently. "We have to shift the load on the thrice-damned rear camel again."

Kamin could see the wooden poles holding the cargo had gone out of alignment around her hump, and the camel was balking at every step, creating a drag on the rest of the string, which in turn upset the camels marching behind them. With a sigh, he went to assist. *At this rate, I'm in for a long two days of travel.*

The caravan ambled along at the speed of the camels, not stopping until midafternoon, when they reached an oasis, and then all the camels and donkeys had to be unloaded and tended to. Several of the ten animals in his string needed salve rubbed into their hides where the cargo harnesses had chafed. *I certainly am earning our passage and hope never to have to do so again.* Rubbing a rag to remove the strong-smelling paste from his hands, Kamin was hot and filthy by the time he was released to seek his tent. Wondering if Nima would be there, fearing she wouldn't be, he was pleasantly surprised to find her waiting inside with a platter of figs, flat bread, several strips of dried meat and a bowl of spiced yogurt. A frothy pitcher of beer and two mugs sat off to the side.

He poured himself a full mug of the liquid and drained it in one sustained gulp. "Dusty work, shepherding a lot of complaining camels all day."

"I brought our dinner," she said. "You might want to take a bath in the oasis pond first." She wrinkled her nose.

"Smell like a camel, do I? No need to mince words." Kamin laughed, rubbing his chin. "I've got stubble as well, but I think it's going to be days before I can shave properly."

"I'll forgive the start of a beard if you take a bath at least." She dipped the bread into the yogurt and bit off a chunk, chewing delicately. "The caravan feeds us well. I'll leave the food here for you."

In the act of stripping off his tunic, Kamin paused. "Where are you off to?"

"Once the camp is completely set up, Andrios has called for a rehearsal. He's created a new story he's telling through dance. He wants my opinion on it, as an Egyptian, representing his future audience." Nima's face fairly glowed with her pleasure in being consulted by the Minoan, and Kamin bit back a cutting remark.

He probably wants more than her opinion.

"Andrios promised to teach me some new acrobatic moves as well. Come and watch, after you've eaten and bathed," she invited.

Kamin grabbed a chunk of the bread. "I wouldn't miss the opportunity." *Time to meet this man Andrios and assess how much of a threat to me he might be when it comes to Nima.* As she skipped from the tent in eager haste, he wished yet again that he wasn't under strict orders of secrecy. The desire to tell Nima everything about himself and settle this issue of a relationship between them was driving him mad. *And despite the fact she was willing to make love to me in the Afterlife, I can't honestly say I know how she feels about me, about staying with me, rather than living her dream of traveling with the dancers. Nothing about the experience in the duat has much relevance here in daily life. We were under the unearthly spell of the place.* He caught a whiff of camel rising from his tunic and wrinkled his nose. *And this situation we're in now has quite a different aspect.*

*****

Later, having taken a bath to rinse off the stink of camel, and with a full belly, Kamin walked toward the far side of the caravan encampment, following the sound of music. He pushed his way through a throng of onlookers and paused, watching Nima in the arms of a Minoan dancer who was evidently in the middle of lifting her into some complex acrobatic maneuver as part of their dance. Hand clenched on the hilt of his sword, Kamin could barely restrain himself from interrupting the scene so intense was his jealousy over the man touching a barely clad Nima—*his* Nima. He acknowledged the unusually possessive thought with a rueful frown.

Such things were never done in Egyptian dance, and he was amazed she'd participate in this. *But she has a daring spirit and a strong thirst for knowledge, especially when it comes to her art. Isn't that part of what I admire about her?* Only the certainty that if he interrupted them in the midst of their lifts and throws she might be physically hurt stopped him from deliberately breaking the pattern of the dance.

Glancing around, he tried to gauge the feeling in the crowd. Ptahnetamun kept a tight grip on his workers, maintained a high level of discipline, but Kamin remembered how aroused and volatile the Hyksos had been while watching Nima. The people here appeared merely interested, appreciative of the skills on display. He relaxed his guard a fraction.

Applause signaled the end of the particular sequence the troupe had been practicing, and the dancers scattered to refresh themselves and rest in what shade there was. Kamin strode into the dusty circle of ground.

Rubbing her face with a damp rag one of the dancers had handed her, Nima broke into a smile. "You came! Did you see that last set of moves? Wasn't it amazing? Oh, let me introduce you to Andrios, the troupe master."

Reluctantly, Kamin shook hands with the man, sensing from his unsmiling face that the dancer was already feeling a rivalry, just as he was. "The acrobatics were interesting. Different."

"Not to your taste, I gather?" Andrios said, eyebrow raised. "Yet Nima dances so well."

"Aye, that she does." Kamin smiled at her. "But she's going to need her strength for travel when we leave the caravan the day after tomorrow."

Nima shook her head, biting her lip. "I gain energy from sharing steps with other dancers, from learning. You don't understand, Kamin, this is a rare opportunity for me."

"And as to your departure," Andrios said, putting his arm around Nima's waist so they stood hip to hip, as if to emphasize they were a team, "I'm doing my best to persuade her to join our troupe, sign a contract with the caravan master." He gave Kamin a somewhat hostile gaze, eyes narrowed. "It's you who are on the run from enemies, as I understand it. Not her."

"Well, to be fair, I was their prisoner, too," Nima said, looking from one man to the other. She sidled a few inches away, breaking the intimate hold Andrios had on her.

Angered by the casual manner in which the troupe master was putting his hands on Nima, Kamin took her elbow and exerted a little pressure. "Can we talk for a moment?" He glared at Andrios. "Privately?"

The Minoan inclined his head a fraction, squeezed Nima close for a heartbeat and walked away, running his hands through the riotous black curls on his head. He called to his dancers. "We'll be starting on the next set of moves in a few minutes."

Tugging her elbow free of his clasp, Nima glared at Kamin. "Are you trying to embarrass me by being rude to him? Like two crowing cocks in the yard, all ruffled feathers and puffed chests and me the hen in the middle. Honestly! I thought you understood how much this encounter with the Minoans meant to me. Surely there's no harm in enjoying myself for a day or two in the midst of our troubles, as long as we're traveling with the caravan anyway. I beg you, please don't diminish my pleasure."

He brought up the least of his concerns as an opener. "They dance so strangely."

"Different than what you're used to, but that's the fun in it for me, new things to learn." She spread her hands wide. "I'm actually *happy*. For a few moments when I'm dancing with them, I manage to forget the awful things that happened to me in the past few weeks. I can just dance, connect with the energy and the flow of movement. And feel free. "

Fear of losing her to the enticements of the troupe drove him to make an unfortunate remark, one he wished he could call back as soon as the words left his lips. "Andrios wants to teach you more than dance steps and simple acrobatics," he said.

"Oh, now we're speaking more plainly. What gives you the right to be jealous about anything I choose to do?" Her eyes sparkled with anger, and she took a deliberate step away from him.

Too late, he realized the quagmire he'd stumbled into. "I only meant—"

"I know what you meant. I'm a grown woman who's been dancing in taverns all her life. I can take care of myself. If you came to make me unhappy, then you can go." Spinning on her heel, Nima made a beeline to where Andrios was waiting, his eyes on her even as he chatted and laughed with the female dancers Kamin had met earlier in the day.

As the Minoan reached to hug Nima and draw her into the conversation, he sent a triumphant glance and a wicked smile in Kamin's direction.

Grinding his teeth, hand clenched on the handle of his belt knife, Kamin left the impromptu dance area, seething at his rival and at himself. *A defeat brought on by my own stupidity. What was it Nima had said? Like two cocks fighting over a hen? She's not the woman to be won in such a fashion, as I well know.* Taking up a position at the perimeter of the crowd, where he'd have a clear view of the dancing when they resumed practicing, he shook his head ruefully. *If she gives me another chance, I've got to be a lot smarter in my wooing strategy.* Nima wasn't paying any attention to him as she chatted animatedly with her new friends, demonstrating a dance step for them. He couldn't begrudge her the happiness she was obviously experiencing but neither could he banish his fear of losing her to the dancing life. *The stakes have never been higher in any fight of my lifetime. If only she gives me the chance, I'll make her other dreams come true, I swear it.* He looked at her again, so at home and accepted in the group of friendly dancers. *But will she offer me that chance?*

CHAPTER SIX

Far too early the next morning, Nima leaned on the stone wall surrounding the well, stifling a yawn and nibbled at a piece of journey bread, waiting for the caravan to push itself into motion. She'd deliberately spent the night away from Kamin again, testing her feelings for him, assessing the reality of what she was about to do. She'd enjoyed her time with the Minoan dancers, not just sharing steps and new moves, but also asking them questions about living and traveling with the caravan.

Andrios and his dancers probably thought she was really considering Ptahn-etamun's offer and were excited, providing advice and encouragement. *And I know Andrios is hoping my curiosity extends to his talents in lovemaking as well.* But she knew she was just playing with the concept, living the nomad artist's life by proxy for a night or two.

The opportunity was opening up too late. Even a few weeks ago, she'd have signed the contract and been gone without a backward glance. *Why didn't I ever at least talk to a caravan master about the possibilities?* Note taken for the future—if there was a future to be had after this Hyksos problem ended—be bold and pursue dreams. No more drifting along.

Bracelets jangling, Thala nudged her in the ribs. "Here comes your man, looking for you."

"Uh huh." Affecting a casual air she didn't really feel, Nima pushed down a little surge of excitement. *I hope he was as upset by our spat yesterday as I was.* She turned to rummage in her sack for some fruit, offering a date to her companion. "Making sure I haven't wandered into Andrios's bed."

"It means something that the soldier was so jealous," Thala said, licking yogurt from her fingers. "He must have feelings for you, my friend. "

"He seemed so bereft when you turned your back on him and ignored him," Mika added, leaning over to grab a fig for herself from the sack.

"And he stayed on the fringe of the crowd the entire evening, watching you dance." Thala nodded, patting Nima on the shoulder. "Actually, he was watching the bystanders more than he paid attention to you, in case the men got out of hand, I think. It must be nice to have such a fearsome warrior looking out for you." She shrugged. "Andrios is a fine troupe master, an excellent dancer, but he'll never settle for any one woman. This soldier of yours acts like a man who's given his heart, perhaps in spite of himself."

"I think we should leave the lovebirds alone," Mika said with a laugh. "In case they want to quarrel again before the inevitable lovemaking heals the anger." Taking one more date, she and Thala strolled away, heading for the dance troupe's wagons.

Shrugging off the girls' lighthearted banter, Nima watched Kamin striding confidently through the lines of camels and the hurrying workers. *What about him captivates me so? He's not like any other soldier I've ever met. Handsome, yes.* She knew he would have drawn her attention in any crowded inn. But looks were only part of the attraction. *Handsome* she could walk away from. Was it his confidence? His skill as a warrior? The way he took such good care of her on the hard trail they followed?

"He treats me like an equal in this adventure," she said out loud. *Not some burden he has to shoulder for honor's sake because I happened to free him.* She'd been acutely conscious of him at her back during the endless senet game, lending her silent strength and support, trusting her to use her skills and win their freedom again. *We're partners. I've never had anything close to trust and true partnership with any other person, and I don't want to give that up.* True, he'd spoken no words of love, although her foolish heart beat faster now just remembering how he'd claimed her as his woman twice in front of the caravan crew. *I know he was only trying to protect me, but perhaps... I'm willing to stay the course and hope.*

Always a gambler!

And he certainly was unhappy with the attention Andrios was giving me.

Nima felt an irrepressible smile curving her lips as Kamin approached, walking fast.

Giving her a bow, as if she was some grand lady at Pharaoh's court, he said, "One of the camels has given birth this morning. Out of season, but the calf appears healthy."

A bit surprised by his choice of topic, she went along with it. "Is that the source of the delay in departure? I wondered."

"Yes, Ptahnetamun doesn't want to abandon a perfectly good camel, so we've waited for the mother to give birth. I—I thought you might like to come see the baby. It's a cute little thing." He rubbed the back of his neck as if suddenly uncomfortable with the notion.

"I'd love to, thank you." She pushed away from the stone wall, and they walked together out of the center of the oasis and down the caravan line.

"I want to apologize for my words last night," he said as soon as they were well away from the cluster of Minoans. "I never meant to spoil your pleasure in the dancing." Brow furrowed, eyes worried, he looked at her. "That's the last thing I would *ever* want to do. It's my nature to protect those who—who mean the most to me, and I let my emotions get the better of my common sense when Andrios provoked me."

"I'm sorry I grew angry in turn," she said. "And he *was* trying to be provoking. I think I'm learning that all troupe masters have certain traits in common. But I can take care of myself."

Kamin nodded. "A fact of which I'm well aware, and one I swear not to forget again. You saved my life twice, after all."

"But I appreciate your care and concern." She couldn't stop herself from smiling at him, and warmth spread through her at the broad grin on his face when he realized she wasn't mad at him this morning.

"Here's my temporary string of camels," he said a moment later, pushing a path through the assembled caravan drivers so Nima could see the baby.

"Oh, how darling!" All gawky long legs, covered in brown fuzz, the newborn camel was struggling to rise from a bed of straw tossed onto the dusty trail, while its mother chewed her cud and seemed unconcerned. Nima tried to move closer. "May I pet him?"

"Sorry, my lady, the calf needs to nurse," said the loadmaster. "We've been delayed far too long already today."

"You can pet him while we load him into a sack after he nurses," Kamin said.

"A sack?"

"The baby can't possibly keep up with the caravan on those spindly legs. We'll make him comfortable in a sack and let the camel in front of the mother carry him, so she can be at ease, keeping the calf in her sight," Kamin explained.

"More from the library of knowledge you keep locked in your head?" she teased, hopping out of the impatient camel drover's way.

Kamin laughed. "Yes, although this particular set of facts I'd hoped never to need again. Camels aren't the most pleasant companions. Give me a chariot and two horses!"

"You are good with those." She nodded, remembering his expert driving the night they'd fled the Hyksos camp.

A little silence fell between them, but not uncomfortable.

"I should take you back to the dancers," he said at length, as it became apparent she wasn't going to have a chance to pet the baby camel any time soon. "Better for you to travel with them than here with me and the camel drovers."

"All right." Nima let him lead her away from the baby camel, which was successfully nursing now.

"About this evening—" Kamin said, not wanting any further misunderstandings to arise between them.

"I want to dance for you," Nima interrupted him. "A private dance," she continued, blushing, not meeting his eyes.

His cock twitched, and he fought to concentrate, not sure he'd heard her correctly. "I only have so much self-control. Are you sure performing for me—and the aftermath—are what you want? You said you didn't do private dances." His heart sank as a new possibility occurred to him. *And does she mean this as a farewell?*

"I might not have another chance to dance for you, to be intimate with you. Traveling with the caravan for a few days has been nothing short of a miracle. The outcome of our journey remains uncertain, hanging on a roll of the dice. Or a toss of the senet sticks," she said with a smile. "I don't expect—or want—you to have self-control. I've chosen to dance for you of my own free will. How you choose to reward me for my skill is up to you." Nima peered up at him coyly from under her lush eyelashes. "A dancer does require a certain amount of audience appreciation to do her best."

Even in the rush of arousal, he fastened on the point that meant more to him even than a private dance and the lovemaking that would follow. He caught her hand and swung her around to face him. "Then you aren't going to sign a contract with Ptahnetamun? Not going north with the dancers, but leaving the caravan tomorrow with me?"

"I'm going with you, soldier, gods know why." She leaned closer and winked. "I think you need me."

"No argument there." He hugged her. "Gods know you'd probably be safer in the caravan than you'll be staying in jeopardy with me, eluding Hyksos at every turn, but the thought of journeying on without you was a heavy burden on my heart." Kamin took a deep breath. "There are things you should know about me, but I'm under stringent orders not to reveal anything until my report is safely delivered to the nomarch. Not even to you. But I swear—"

She put her finger on his lips to silence him, then framed his face with her hands as she said in a low voice, "I know you're an honorable man. I know you treat me as your equal." A smile lit up her face. "I know you have three younger sisters who probably adore you, and I don't need to know anymore right now. " Going on tiptoe, she kissed him on the lips, ignoring the whistles of the nearby drovers. Strolling on, hand in hand with Kamin, she said, "There are things I must do if I'm to dance properly for you tonight. I'm hoping the troupe will be able to provide what I need. "

"All *I* need is you," Kamin said, kissing her cheek.

"Gratifying to hear, soldier, but I'd like to present a better show than just myself humming, dancing in this shabby dress." Eyebrows drawn together in a frown, she picked at the skirt fabric. "Not suitable for a performance of the kind I have in mind."

"We've no deben or coin," he reminded her.

"The troupe shared a few of their coins from the first night's performance with me. And I've done a bit of gaming. No senet for high stakes," she rushed to assure him. "But I do know how to win at other games."

They'd arrived at the well, and the dancers called to her to join them.

Kamin kissed her hand. "Until tonight then."

*****

After his eagerness and impatience all day during the caravan's march, their tent was empty when he stepped inside that evening. He'd stopped at the water casks first and used up most of his daily ration in a rushed bath, so he wouldn't offend Nima by coming to her smelling like a camel. Splashing the tepid water over himself, he thought longingly of the baths at home. *I must be getting soft. Never worried about my grooming on a mission before.*

Kamin's chuckle ended, and the breath whooshed out of his chest as he surveyed the tent worriedly for signs of Nima. *Where is she? I wasn't exactly expecting her to be lying naked on the pillows, but certainly I thought to find her waiting.* Someone pushed into the tent behind him, and he pivoted, a little off guard, hand on his knife hilt, but the newcomer was Thala, the Minoan dancer.

"Don't worry about your woman," the woman said. "She's obtained a slightly larger tent for her, uh, performance tonight. I've been sent to guide you to the right place."

Wondering how much cheating at games of chance Nima had done in the last two days to arrange the evening in a way that seemed suitable to her, Kamin followed Thala outside and farther down the line of tents until they paused at a larger blue enclosure, set up a bit away from the main encampment. Thala led him inside.

Again, there was no sign of Nima. His anxiety thrummed through his body. *Where is she?*

"She requests you to take your ease." The dancer gestured toward a pile of pillows and cushions against the far wall of the tent. "I'll leave you with your dinner—stew with steamed grain, almonds, dates, beer. Nima will arrive shortly to entertain you." Grinning, she left him alone in the tent, carefully closing the fabric panels behind her.

Wondering whose tent this was and how Nima had wangled their use of it for the night, Kamin set aside his weapons, keeping them close at hand in case of emergency. Surveying the food, he choked down one bite of stew then pushed the bowl away on the low table. *I'm not eating without Nima.*

The curtain between the halves of the tent twitched, drawing his attention. A moment later, Nima slipped through the narrow space. Barefoot, she was dressed in an unusual outfit, constructed from pieces of shimmering red fabric, cleverly draped and knotted strategically on her body to show flashes of skin, tantalizing glimpses of her sensuous figure. The costume was accented with filmy scarves. A jeweled sash rode low on her hips, anchoring the slit skirt, golden tassels bobbing with every step. Her jet-black hair was braided tightly in classic Egyptian tradition, waist length, soft end brushing the luscious curve of her bottom.

Inhaling sharply, Kamin leaned back, his cock already rising to strain against his loincloth, balls drawing up tight to his body. *Gods, she's beautiful.*

Nima came to the center of the tent, eyes focused on the floor, then chimed her finger cymbals once and lifted her head, eyes seeking his face. Kamin swallowed hard. Raising both arms above her head, fingers cupped as if to catch raindrops, she assumed a classic dancer's pose, one foot planted solidly, on tiptoe with the other. A moment later, unseen musicians seated in the outer chamber played the first measures of music. Kamin heard a hand drum, flutes, other instruments he didn't recognize, playing a version of a tune known as a standard in taverns along the Nile. *She must have practiced with them on the march, during the day.*

Keeping her eyes locked on his face, Nima rose effortlessly onto her toes, signaling the beginning of his private dance. He couldn't have looked away if the entire Hyksos army had burst into the tent. She undulated her hips in time to the music, swirling two of the scarves through the air in sinuous arcs, now concealing, now revealing. As the pace of the song altered and switched to a subtle dance pattern, she dropped the sheer fabric triangles, moving her feet in rapid but tiny steps, translating to an enticing display of the abilities of her limber core muscles and hips. Time and again the sparkling belt drew Kamin's eyes to her pelvis as she moved in sensuous patterns. The beat rose and fell, accented by the throbbing drum, and she thrust her hips and pelvis in sync with the music, now this way, then the other direction, maintaining the amazing gliding step. Every few measures of the song, she would allow the upper portion of her body to sway, forward, back, sideways, breasts bobbing against the shiny fabric restraining them, as if she were offering herself for his feasting then coyly withdrawing before he could taste.

She made a slow turn as she danced, until she no longer faced him. Her hips moved rapidly in tight circles, first to the right and then to the left, in time to the music, while her hands wove patterns in the air. The music called her to a series of incredibly intricate steps, emphasizing her grace and her muscle control. Revolving to him again as the dance proceeded, Nima continued the erotic movements, the music adding intensity to the dance.

Aroused to the point of physical pain, Kamin strove for self-control. Shifting his hips involuntarily, he imagined himself plunging his aching manhood into her, her strong dancer's muscles sheathing him, drawing his cock deeper into her body. Her dance was a skillful blend of raw sensuality with the elegance and refined movements seen only in high temples. He'd never beheld the like before. Oh, he'd been at performances by the best dancers in Thebes. He'd even had such dancers performing primarily for him, as Nima did tonight, but there the resemblance to anything he'd ever before experienced stopped. Dancing for all men with consummate skill, Theban dancers were professionals, smiling radiantly and impartially for the entire audience. Only the richest or most highly born men could expect an invitation to bed a top-tier Theban dancer.

As she performed for him alone, Nima's smile was genuine, not practiced. The delectable hint of shyness, the faint blush on her cheeks said she was inviting him and *only* him to make love to her.

More scarves, then the skirt and jeweled belt fell to the tent floor as she wove her magic dance, until she was in her breast band and a tiny loincloth. Kamin could hardly restrain himself from leaving the pillows to take her in his arms and plunge his cock into her before the dance ended. His blood raced. The slight amount of coverage on her breasts and mound as she danced was more erotic than if she were nude. He imagined himself pinning her beneath him, ripping off the fabric, setting his lips to her most private places while she writhed in pleasure.

Nima opened the dance up for a few measures as the music slowed, the sensuality heightened, swirling in her dance space, arms moving languorously to frame her face, her body... The drum beat faster, and she twirled, cymbals chiming on her fingertips to punctuate each movement, then suddenly the climax was reached, the dance was done.

Head bowed, Nima sank to the floor, one arm extended to him, palm up.

All his senses on fire, Kamin surged from the pillows, bending to take her hand and pull her into his arms. He kissed her, crushing her body to his, hands roaming over her back, the perfect curve of her bottom. He unfastened the simple knot on the upper garment and yanked it out from between them, his hand going to caress and savor the soft curves of her breasts. "Gods, woman, you've driven me insane."

She peeked at him through her long lashes. "My dance pleased you?"

"I've never seen anything to rival the performance you gave." Picking her up so she wrapped her legs around his waist, as he had fantasized so many times since they'd met, he carried her the few steps to the pillows and laid her tenderly on the soft surface. Tearing off his confining robes, he unwound his loincloth to let his erection spring free.

She lay on the pillows, smiling at him, only the scanty loincloth remaining to her. Kamin's knees trembled ever so slightly with the sheer effort it took to restrain himself from coming just admiring her body displayed for him. Nima reached up one hand to him. "Is something wrong?"

"No, everything is perfect. You're so beautiful, I want to take my time, admire every inch of you." He lay on the pillows beside her, cupping one breast with his hand, relishing the weight and the satin feel of her skin, kneading the nipple until it was a bud, then lowering his head to tease and suckle. She held him close, one hand tracing the pattern of his muscles, gliding over his chest, past his waist, to curl possessively around his jutting cock.

Kamin groaned, raising his head. "Nima, *stop*. Your dance has me so hot, I'll finish before I can make love to you properly if you keep touching me."

"We have all night," she answered, rubbing his cock in a slow, circular motion from root to tip. "Although I can't perform an encore, since Andrios only lent me the services of his musicians for the space of one song. Grudgingly."

"A repeat performance of your amazing dance would probably kill me right now." He captured her mouth again. Sliding one hand along her body, enjoying the feel of her supple dancer's muscles under his palm, he caressed the curve of her hip before sliding his fingers under the edge of her loincloth, parting the silky curls and finding to his delight and relief that she was wet and slick. The discovery was so pleasing, arousing him even more, it was a moment's work to rip the fabric away from her body, Nima lifting her hips to make the process easier.

Pushing her thighs open, he slid down her body, admiring the effect of his darkly tanned hands on her soft thighs and exploring her with his tongue, licking, savoring the essence of woman. She tunneled her fingers in his hair and arched her body as his skillful massaging of her most private places brought her closer to climax. Convulsing under him, she screamed his name. As her tremors of pleasure diminished, he withdrew, taking her in his arms again and gazing tenderly into her face.

"Good?" He kissed her on the lips, smoothing her hair away from her face.

"Mmm." She nodded, one hand trailing down his back in a light caress, leg hooked over his.

"Well, then, as this is finally the right place and the right time, let me improve on the beginning we've made."

He reached to guide his throbbing cock into her body, now thoroughly ready to accept his girth. The sensation against the head of his shaft was intense as her soft sheath expanded, and he had to stop for a moment, breathing deeply, to keep himself from thrusting hard and coming too soon. Impatient now, she shimmied her dancer's hips a bit and drew him further inside, clenching and releasing, in the most erotic pulsation he'd ever felt.

Closing her eyes, Nima apparently concentrated all her attention on goading him past the point of no return. Her hands stroked his back while her legs were locked, holding him, urging him to plunge deeper. She was hot, slick against his hard cock, and Kamin stopped resisting the demands of his body, plunging deep, then almost withdrawing in a rhythm that intensified as his control slipped. She met him move for move, her trained core muscles contracting in ways he'd never experienced before, massaging his cock as he penetrated her until he found release in one long, exuberant moment. From the way she was moving against his-still rigid shaft, he could tell her own pleasure was not quite complete. Reaching with one hand to where their warm, sweaty bodies joined, he found the tiny pearl he knew could send a woman over the edge and massaged firmly as he thrust in and out.

Nima's second orgasm was even more powerful than the first, paroxysms of muscle tremors driving him to another release of his own, jetting his seed deep into her.

Spent, he collapsed, rolling with her in his arms so they lay together on their sides, joined, hot and sweaty, but satisfied. Nima's eyes were closed. Tenderly, Kamin traced his finger over the apple of her cheek, bringing his hand to her breast and circling the nipple with his fingertips. He lowered his head, catching the rosy tip gently in his teeth before he suckled, his tongue swirling around the sensitive spot. She squirmed, trying to get even closer to him.

Releasing the nipple, he blew a soft breeze across the pebbled surface. Nima shivered.

Raising his head, he met her gaze, and words he'd never uttered before came from deep within his soul. "I love you."

Her face softened into a tender smile. "And I love you, my brave soldier."

"I've longed to hear that declaration on your lips." He rolled over, semi-erect cock sliding out of Nima's warmth. He positioned her with her head pillowed on his broad shoulder and pulled the nearest blanket over her. Hooking one leg across his thighs, Nima ran her hand across his taut abdomen, tracing the muscles, then sliding her hand to his cock. She gently massaged his balls for a moment, rolling them in her hand, before stroking the sensitive area directly behind them. Kamin took in a long breath, pleasure tingling in his every nerve, as she paid fascinated attention to his manhood. Nima changed her position, moving to pillow her head on his thigh, reaching to take possession of him. Holding his shaft firmly in her hands, she licked the head in a swirling motion, softly blowing air across the sensitive surface as he had done to her body earlier. He clenched his fists in her hair, restraining himself. He wanted her mouth on him more than he wanted to breathe, but the choice had to be hers.

Nima took him in her mouth, lush lips holding him in place as her tongue played. The warm wetness of her mouth and skillful swirling of her tongue on his cock was exquisite torture.

Grasping at the last shreds of self-control, Kamin fought not to release his seed no matter how his body strained. His voice was hurried, a bit breathless. "Nima, I'm going to come if you don't stop."

She applied the suction of lips and tongue to him one moment longer before raising her head and licking her lips, smiling. Her hand stroked the length of his throbbing shaft, applying light but teasing pressure.

Kamin pulled her up and positioned her under him in one rapid motion, seeking the hot core of her body as they moved together, knowing she was more than ready to accept him again. He brought her to climax at the instant he himself was losing control, and they locked around each other in a fierce, passionate embrace. He reveled in her pleasure even as he was satisfied.

"You, my dancer, are an amazing woman. I've never met anyone to equal you," Kamin said, kissing her thoroughly before rising to get a pitcher of water and cloths stacked in the corner of the tent. The water was warm, and he bathed Nima's body with loving care as she drowsed. He washed himself rapidly and rejoined her on the pillows, curling up together as close as they could get.

"You were more than worth waiting for," he whispered in her ear.

Pulling the cover up over them both, Nima made a small "mmm" sound of satisfaction and contentment as she drifted to sleep, nestled against him.

CHAPTER SEVEN

In the morning they made love again, quickly, with no time to properly savor the moment, as the sounds of the caravan preparing to leave could be heard all around them. As he lay back on the pillows, Kamin stroked Nima's hair away from her flushed face and kissed her cheek. "Not exactly the way I wished to greet the morning, my love, but I have a feeling if we don't leave this bed soon, they'll start taking the tent down around us."

She kissed him back. "Agreed."

They both got up, searching out their clothing, and made hasty work of dressing.

"Must you work again today?" she asked while he was buckling on his weapons.

"No. I told the loadmaster I'd only give him two days of labor, since we depart the caravan midday." He held out his hand. "Shall we go see the baby camel after grabbing some breakfast rations?"

As they strolled out of the tent, four men standing by immediately brushed past them and began taking the poles and fabric down. Nima blushed a little but kept her head high as Kamin escorted her away from the crew. While he gathered some dates and hard rolls from the caravan cook for their morning meal, Nima returned the borrowed clothes to Thala. Kamin watched from afar as she exchanged hugs with various dancers. Munching on his breakfast roll, he tried not to grin at the obviously sour look on Andrios's face.

He held his tongue when she rejoined him. *A wise man learns from his mistakes.*

*****

They'd been marching for several hours, hand in hand, chatting about inconsequential things, when suddenly the rhythm of the caravan stuttered, camels ahead of them jerking to a stop with much cursing on the part of the drovers. There was mild chaos.

Kamin stopped, looking around with his eyes narrowed. "I don't like this. The one thing a caravan never does all day is come to a halt before the appointed hour or at the desired destination. Even if a camel died under its load, the others would be walked around it. Something must be seriously wrong."

Nima clutched his arm. "Could it be the Hyksos?"

"Perhaps." He checked the nearest drovers but didn't see anyone he recognized, much less someone he'd trust with Nima's safety. "I should go reconnoiter, but I hate to leave you here alone."

"I have my dagger." She showed him.

"Someone comes." He shoved her behind him and drew his sword.

"It's only Thala." Sighing in relief, Nima stepped away to greet her friend.

Face set in worried lines, Thala was swathed in her cloak, walking as fast as she could without breaking into an attention-drawing run. "You've got to flee," she said as soon as she drew near. "There's a party of Hyksos determined to search the caravan. Their leader is a man by the name of Amarkash, and he seems sure you're here." She thrust a parcel at Nima. "Water, some food. A map. Ptahnetamun is trying to delay the enemy commander, saying they've no right to search his caravan. He passed the word to his men to make as much confusion with the camel strings as they could, while I came to find you."

"But he'll have to submit eventually," Kamin said. "He won't get embroiled in a fight on our behalf."

Nodding at his assessment of the situation, Thala gave Nima a hug. "Ptahnetamun said to tell you to go due east for an hour or two until you reach a large rock formation taller than two men and then the map will help you find the actual track he spoke of, the one that has wells and an oasis. Quickly now, you haven't a moment to waste."

Kamin shook her hand. "Thank you for everything."

"I hope we meet again someday, in better circumstances," Thala answered. "And another thing you should know. The Hyksos have one of their filthy priests with them."

"A priest of Qemtusheb? Are you sure?" Kamin was dismayed by the news.

"I recognize the robes." She spat. "I've seen them before, when we traveled outside of Egypt. They practice human sacrifice and black magic so you must avoid him at all costs."

"Where did he come from?" Nima's voice shook, and her eyes widened in horror.

Shrugging, Kamin shook his head. "I wouldn't be surprised if another group of Hyksos has joined Amarkash, like the men who captured me did." He held out his hand. "Let's go."

Staying low and using every ounce of cover he could find in the barren wasteland, Kamin led Nima away from the caravan, expecting any moment to hear enemy war cries, but luck or the gods favored them.

*****

The sun rose higher, and the day heated up inexorably as their journey continued. After a while, Kamin slowed the pace, glancing at Nima occasionally to make sure she was doing all right. He brought them to a halt in the shade of a few gnarled, spindly trees and handed her the water skin.

Before packing the water away, he kissed her, licking the water droplets from her lips. "We'd better keep moving." He offered her his hand, and reluctantly she rose to step away from the meager shade.

Pausing in midstep, Nima jerked her head in the direction they had come. "Did you hear something?"

He loosened his sword in its sheath. "No. What do you think you heard?"

Hesitating, Nima struggled to describe the sound with certainty. "Like a dog's howl," she said finally. "Far away, though."

"Perhaps a band of nomads is in the vicinity. One of their herd dogs. We're traveling toward some water source, according to Ptahnetamun," he reminded her.

"No dog I ever heard howled in such a tone." Nima shook her head.

"I didn't hear the noise, but as long we don't hear it again, I don't think we need be concerned." Kamin squeezed her hand in reassurance, but left his sword ready to draw rapidly if necessary.

They hiked, soon increasing their speed to an easy run, Kamin holding his pace to hers.

Every couple of minutes, he checked the empty landscape behind them, walking backward for eight or nine paces, scanning the horizon.

After the fifth time he performed this ritual, Nima challenged him. "What's wrong?"

He frowned. "I can't shake the feeling something is following us. Even if we haven't heard howling for a few minutes now."

Eyes wide, she glanced at the horizon behind them. "Why would anything follow us, except for the Hyksos?"

He rolled his shoulders. "I don't know. The common predators out here on the open desert should be afraid to tangle with humans, at least in broad daylight."

Cutting across his words was a definite howl, from more than one animal's throat. Kamin gave Nima a gentle push to urge her to run, sprinting hot on her heels. Not breaking stride, Kamin unslung the bow from his shoulder and nocked an arrow to the string, ready to defend his woman.

The terrain subsided abruptly, leading to a small stream running through the narrow vee at the bottom of the hill, before rising again on the other side. Kamin helped Nima balance as she skidded down the slope, the shale and gravel loose under her feet. At the bottom, they waded through the shallow water hastily and began the strenuous climb up the other side.

Nima glanced back the way they'd just come and a scream tore from her throat. Losing her balance on the crumbling hillside, she clutched at Kamin to keep from tumbling all the way to the bottom, ending with a dunking in the stream. One arm around her waist, he checked to see what was behind them to frighten her so, and his stomach clenched.

A huge dog-like creature watched them from across the river divide. The head was unusually small for the body and round, with a pointed muzzle and pointed ears, pricked up as it stared at them. The animal's back sloped to muscular hindquarters, and its hair or mane stood upright along the spine, its bushy tail wagging slowly as it bared fangs at them. Stripes ran along the creature's spine, with spots on its hindquarters. A second joined the original animal. By Kamin's estimate, they both stood about four feet tall at the shoulders, and each probably weighed as much as he did.

"What are they?" Nima whispered.

"Could be hyenas, although I've never seen any so big. The beast has the appearance of some kind of demon spawn—see the reddish eyes?" Kamin gave her a gentle push. "Keep going. Get to the top of the hill."

Obediently, she adjusted her burden and took a few steps.

The animal snarled, red, viscous drool dripping from its bared fangs onto the sand. It gathered its haunches as if to spring across the small valley at them. Kamin lifted the bow and took aim. *It can't believe it can make such a leap.* No sooner than the foreboding idea flashed through his mind, then the hyena launched itself into the air, clearly possessing the power and agility to jump the distance. Kamin shot his arrow, striking the beast between the eyes.

Moving with practiced skill and speed, he nocked another arrow, aimed and shot while the hyena shrieked defiance and crumpled in midair. The animal landed hard on the incline below him, red, rage-filled eyes locked onto his, front paws scrabbling at the dirt as if to pull itself toward its prey. Kamin shot again, hitting the center of the throat. The hyena fell on its side, sliding into the stream, where it twitched once before dying.

Black ooze foamed from the animal's wounds, eating into the ground, and where it had fallen into the stream, the water boiled away, noxious steam rising to the sky. Keeping his eyes on the second hyena while he climbed the hill in a sideways motion, like a crab, Kamin made his retreat, bow at the ready.

Nima caught his arm when he reached the top. "Did you see what happened when it died?"

He nodded, moving her behind him. Lifting its head, the other hyena howled, a long mournful cry, then loped away, back across the dunes.

"Killing its pack mate must have scared the creature off," Nima said.

"Not likely." Kamin checked the carcass in the stream, which continued to deteriorate, becoming mangy fragments of skin and gray bones. "At least they *can* be killed."

Renewed howling from more than one throat sounded in the distance.

"Oh, goddess, there must be a whole pack of them," Nima moaned.

"We need to run." Kamin suited action to the words, pushing her ahead of him. "We've got to find somewhere defensible. If they catch us on the open plain, we're done for."

Nima risked one quick, sidelong glance at him as she ran. "How many arrows do you have left?"

"Not enough. It took three to bring the first one down."

Nima sprinted, Kamin falling slightly behind to play rearguard. The howling sounded closer, an excited, frenzied tone to the call. Tapping her shoulder to gain her attention, Kamin pointed. "Head for the small rock formation to the left. It's the only thing of any significance anywhere. We can fight them off from there."

He slowed, falling behind, taking his archer's stance and letting an arrow fly. Stumbling dangerously, Nima risked a glance behind her, then tried to run even faster toward the jutting rocks.

The pack caught up to them snapping at their heels, flanking them as they ran. Kamin shot to cripple, trying to reduce the numbers and prevent the animals from getting in front and blocking their escape route. The pack stopped in yelping confusion, milling around their injured mates, while Kamin and Nima sprinted the last few yards to the rock formation. First one, then another hyena trotted after them, lengthening their strides to catch up.

Slinging the bow over his shoulder, Kamin threw his packs onto the rocks and gave Nima a boost to the potential safety of the boulders. Bolder and faster than the rest, one hyena darted forward and jumped, catching her by the ankle and dragging her screaming to the dirt. She landed hard, flat on her back. Kamin's dagger was in his hand in the blink of an eye, and he plunged it deep into the animal's side, through the heart. Taking a deep breath, hooking his hands under the beast's chest, he threw the carcass away from Nima, using the dead beast as a weapon to topple another oncoming hyena as it tried to spring at him.

Bending, he jerked her up from the ground, maneuvering her onto the first level of the rock formation, where she landed on all fours with a grunt. Kamin clawed his way up to stand beside her.

"Come on, we must get higher. We've seen how they can jump." He got his hand under her elbow and brought her to her feet.

Screaming in pain, Nima collapsed. Kamin lifted her in his arms and precariously climbed further onto the rock formation. A moment after he left the first plateau, the hyenas were making unsuccessful attempts to leap onto the surface. The howling and barking were deafening.

Kamin got to the next nearly flat area of the rocks and set Nima by the wall, where he could defend her. Taking a quick glance to make sure the hyenas were still stymied by the rocks, he knelt beside her. "What's wrong? How badly did the creature hurt you?"

"My foot, my ankle," she gasped through streams of tears.

"Let me see, move your hands." Kamin whistled as he scrutinized her injuries more closely, heart sinking.

Black streaks ran from the bleeding gashes up her leg under the skin, toward her knee. *Some kind of poison in their bite? How are we going to counteract such vileness?* White-faced, Nima appeared on the verge of throwing up or passing out or both. Quickly, he tore a piece from his cloak and poured water on the cloth, gently cleansing the wounds. "Apparently, the beast didn't clamp down at full strength."

"Hard enough." Biting her lip, Nima swayed.

"You still have a foot," Kamin pointed out in grim tones as he tore another strip to bandage her wound and stop the bleeding. "The pack's behavior has been odd, as if they aren't trying to kill us. Once the beast had you, neither it nor its companions moved in for the death blow."

"Thank the gods." Brushing her hand across her forehead, Nima pushed loose strands of hair aside.

He craned his head and listened for a moment. "It's too quiet. Can you finish tying this bandage? I need to see what they're up to."

"I'm fine, go." Nima knotted the cloth at her ankle above the bone.

When he walked cautiously to the edge of the small plateau, Kamin was greeted by a renewed chorus of unearthly howls. The twelve remaining animals paced and circled at the foot of the rock formation. The corpses of the ones he'd shot or stabbed were bleeding out the black ooze and decomposing. Returning to Nima's side, he knelt, pulling her into a slightly off-balance embrace.

She leaned into him for a moment before kissing his cheek. "What do we do now? How do we escape?"

Good news first. She's pretty fragile right now. "The pack has been whittled to twelve," he said.

"Formidable odds, even if they aren't trying to kill us. Maiming is apparently within their purview." She grimaced.

He considered what he'd seen of the pack, restlessly pacing and howling on the ground below them. "These aren't normal desert hyenas. Such creatures are smaller, not as aggressive."

"And don't bleed black ooze," Nima added. "So, where did these come from?"

"I'm thinking black magic, called up by Qemtusheb's priest, the one Thala warned us about at the caravan encampment this morning." Kamin eyed the bandage. *Had her wounds stopped bleeding yet?*

Nima averted her eyes with a shudder as he lifted the edge of the cloth. "Black magic. Are you serious?"

He nodded. "I've seen manifestations before, when the Usurper Pharaoh ruled. "

She wrinkled her forehead in puzzlement. "But why did the priest send these creatures after us?"

"To track us, pen us somewhere until the Hyksos can follow his magic to our location." Kamin shrugged. "Amarkash must be getting desperate to catch us since we've managed to keep one step ahead of him all this time."

Rubbing her arms, Nima shivered. "We can't stay here, then."

"No." He stood, going to where he'd tossed his quiver. It took a depressingly short time to tally his resources. Showing her the quiver, he said, "Five arrows left. And twelve hyenas. Even if I cripple one with every shot, I can't hope to defeat the final seven in hand-to-hand combat."

*****

Picking up one of the arrows, Nima ran the stiff, brindled feathers through her fingers. "How long do you think we have till the Hyksos arrive?"

He took the arrow back, placing it with the other four. "Probably not too long, since they have chariots."

A familiar keening sounded overhead. Checking the sky, Kamin watched a falcon drifting on the thermals.

Following the direction of the bird's cry, she asked, "Do you think Horus will help us?"

Shading his eyes, Kamin regarded the bird. "He's certainly come to our aid before." The hyenas set up a renewed chorus of angry howls below, apparently stirred to a frenzy by the appearance of the falcon.

"I wish I had a patron goddess to call upon," Nima fretted, fingering the clay bead on her amulet. "Divine assistance would be helpful right now."

Reaching to lay his hand over hers on the bead, Kamin had a question. "Didn't you say your mother beseeched her goddess for one future intervention on your behalf?"

"Yes, but I don't believe her plea was granted." She frowned, withdrawing her hand and smoothing her hair with a nervous gesture. "I told you, I screamed my throat raw, appealing for help the night I was captured in Hebenar, and received no divine aid."

He captured her hand again, lacing his fingers with hers. "These things have to be asked for in the right way, sweetheart. Great Ones can be inaccessible unless approached carefully. I swore an oath to Pharaoh and to Horus, and the god and I have a long history, which is probably why he's been so willing to assist to a degree."

"I don't even know which goddess to appeal to," Nima answered crossly. *Is my lack of knowledge fated to doom us? Why didn't I ever press the issue with her?* Because she'd been a child and her mother had had a tenuous hold on life, so fragile that even a child knew not to raise certain topics. Tears blurred her vision. "My mother never uttered the Great One's name, much less explained how to invoke her."

He hugged her. "Are you willing to try an appeal now?"

How can I refuse, when not only my life but his depends on this chance? Resting her head against his chest, Nima nodded once. "I'll do anything you ask of me."

"I was an observer at a ceremony for Renenutet, the snake goddess, once," Kamin said. "And clearly your amulet relates to one of her aspects."

Shutting her eyes for a moment, Nima shuddered. "Yes, but I'm terrified of snakes."

"If the goddess is attuned to you and if she sends her serpents to aid us, they won't turn on you, I swear. What do we have to lose?" He held her away from him, gazing into her face.

I must look at death's door, his face is so worried. "Magic for magic." Nima smiled weakly, hoping to reassure him. "What do we do?"

"I'll have to cut the amulet off." Reaching for his knife, Kamin raised one eyebrow, waiting for her permission.

Extending her arm, Nima swallowed hard. "If this doesn't work, I can restring the bead later." *Assuming there is a later for us.*

Carefully, he inserted the tip of the blade under the knotted black leather cords and slashed the bracelet free, catching the clay bead as it fell. "Do we have any bread left?"

"You're hungry at a time like this?" Reaching for the packs, she rummaged through the contents, snatching a piece of the caravan cook's flat bread to offer him.

"Renenutet is a goddess of grain and harvests. Bread is the closest to a proper offering we can get on this rock." Holding the bead carefully, Kamin rose and walked to the edge of the rock shelf, checking on the hyenas. A chorus of shrieking sounds rose as he peered over the precipice. "Still prowling. I have no real hope of their giving up and slinking away."

"Sounds like they're laughing at us," Nima said, rubbing her bare wrist. "Like demons, enjoying our predicament. What do we do now?"

Setting the bread in the sunniest spot on the rock, Kamin laid the bead in the center, pushing it into the soft bread and coiling the broken ends of the black thong in a circle. "I need one drop of your blood, sweetheart, so the Great One hears the call through your bond with her—"

"I keep telling you there's no bond, no link, nothing." Nima held out her hand, closing her eyes. She gritted her teeth. "Go ahead, prick my finger."

Nothing happened. Puzzled, braced for the pinprick, she opened her eyes to find Kamin oddly hesitant. Bewildered, she studied his face for a moment. "What?"

Pointing the knife at her ankle, he explained his insight. "I'm thinking a drop of your blood from where the hyena bit you might be better. Then the goddess would be aware of the black magic as well."

Nima picked at the edge of the bandages he'd just applied. "You have a certain grim logic to this insane idea, soldier. Should I be concerned how much you know about black magic?" Removing the makeshift bandage, she gazed at him with a furrowed brow and wrinkled nose.

Wincing in obvious sympathy, he studied her foot as the bandages fell away. "I'll try not to hurt you."

"The whole foot hurts and throbs, so don't worry about one more prick." She shut her eyes tight as he gently touched the tip of the knife to one of the angry, long, red slashes left by the hyena's fangs and got a few drops of her blood on the blade. The black lines had not progressed much further up her leg, for which she was grateful, but they were a jarring, disquieting occurrence nonetheless.

Sharp pain for a brief moment, then Kamin stood. "I'm done. Cover the wound up again."

Hastily, she wrapped the cloth over the gashes and bruises, tying a neat little knot.

As Kamin moved the knife slowly over the bead, Nima watched first one then two drops of the ruby blood fall onto the raised snake on the bead's surface. The red ran to cover the entire bead without dripping off the edges. Kamin laid the knife aside and spread his hands out, palms up. "Great One Renenutet, we pray most earnestly for you to send us thy servants, the black cobras of the rocks, to kill the hyenas waiting below. The beasts were released to hunt us by priests of Qemtusheb, ruler of demons and enemy of Egypt. We ask for the one intervention Nima's mother begged for, when she left your service so many years ago. Our need is dire, and Egypt's fate may rest on our shoulders."

Eyebrows raised, hand extended toward her, he nodded expectantly.

Pure panic froze Nima's vocal cords for a moment. *I don't know any chants! What does he want me to add?* She swallowed past the lump in her throat, licked her lips. "Please, if my mother meant anything to you, as a dancer, as your priestess, help Kamin and me now," Nima said.

Riding the thermals overhead, the falcon let out a fierce cry and flew into the glare of the sun as she raised her head to watch him.

A thin tendril of black smoke spiraled from the bead. Kamin half lifted Nima away from the spot as first the bead, then the bread burst into angry purple-black flames. Writhing in the fire's grasp, the leather thongs grew, splitting in two then splitting again, lengthening, fattening and spreading beyond the circle of the offering, in a tangle of tails. Nima screamed as eight black cobras raised their heads from the center of the fire circle, sinuously weaving and entwining around each other, red eyes gleaming, black tongues flicking. Hood pulsating, a ninth cobra, black like the others but with a golden head, reared four feet off the surface of the rock. The snake extricated itself from the tangle of lesser reptiles, slithering toward Nima, head weaving from side to side.

She scooted over the rough stone, heart pounding against her ribs, mouth dry, dizziness assailing her. Grabbing her by the shoulders, Kamin held her tight. "It's the goddess, come at our request. Don't panic now. You've got to face her, tell her what we need. Renenutet won't grant any appeal just from me." He gave her a little shake. "Falcons and snakes are sworn enemies."

Plainly listening to his words, the cobra swung its head, studying him for a moment with cold, red-faceted eyes, then hissed loudly and continued to advance on Nima.

She shook in his arms, digging her nails into him, but met the snake's regard. "Please, Great One, we need your help to kill the hyenas waiting below, so we can escape before the enemy arrives. We must carry our news to the nomarch so he can defend Egypt."

Advancing in tiny increments, the snake's flickering ruby tongue touched Nima's parted lips, the feathery touch leaving behind spreading coolness, a taste of vanilla and honey in her mouth. Then the goddess retreated, hissing and spitting, and slithered down the rocks toward the pack of hyenas, her minions going behind her like a rippling black brook. Nima collapsed against Kamin, trying to stop herself from trembling.

"I have to help," he said urgently. "We can't ask for aid and not fight for ourselves." Setting her aside, he gathered up his sword, bow and the five arrows. "Wait here, pray. I'll come for you as soon as I can."

"Kamin!" She caught his hand, and he ducked his head to kiss her before scrambling out of sight on the rocky trail in the direction the snakes had gone. Avoiding the black circle of the burnt offering, Nima dragged herself across the plateau, reaching the edge in time to see her beloved launch himself at two hyenas, sword raised to decapitate.

The falcon came screaming out of the sky at high speed to attack another hyena, sinking its claws into the repulsive head and doing tremendous damage with its hooked beak. Coiling and twining around the rest of the pack, the black snakes drove fangs deep into mangy gray-brown fur. Much howling and whining filled the air. Kamin cursed steadily as he hacked at the beasts with his sword, and the falcon shrieked defiance.

Nima covered her ears but couldn't look away, not while her warrior was in danger. Another hyena slunk from behind the rocks, launching itself at Kamin's unprotected back. Nima screamed a warning, but the golden-headed snake and the hawk both threw themselves into the creature's path, bringing it to its knees inches shy of the intended target.

Staggering away from his kills, Kamin leaned on a rock outcropping, surveying the field of battle. All the hyenas were dead or dying. Then he raised his eyes, giving her a weary wave. "I'll be up in a moment to assist you in the descent, all right?"

"Yes, fine." Nima's attention was all for the field of battle, the hyenas melting into pools of oily black. Slithering from all corners of the torn-up ground, the nine snakes converged, a writhing column, the golden-headed snake corkscrewing to the top and pivoting its massive head to stare directly at Nima. Purple flames burst into life, devouring the cobras and, a moment later, they were gone. Raising a be-ringed hand in farewell and possibly a blessing, a snake-headed woman, crowned by a sun disk and two black feather plumes, her golden sheath dress glimmering, stood on the plain for one heartbeat before she, too, faded away.

Tears streaming down her cheeks, Nima collapsed into a boneless heap.

*****

Wearily, Kamin trudged up the narrow trail to the ledge to find Nima weeping. Distressed, he embraced her. "Sweetheart, it's all right. We can escape this trap now."

She shook her head, shoving her hair aside and wiping tears from her cheeks backhanded. "I'm not crying about any of this. I'm crying for my mother. She'd be so proud to know the goddess came to aid me as promised. How can I ever thank you for drawing Renenutet here to intervene?"

Holding her close to his heart, he kissed her tenderly. "I only provided the right enticements to attract the Great One's attention. She came for you."

"I wish my mother could have seen the goddess. I wish she could know—"

An awful suspicion took root in Kamin's mind. "When your mother died, were there any ceremonies for her?"

Straightening, Nima wiped her eyes and tried a wavering smile. "No. She had no deben. She—she drank a lot of wine and beer daily, with each meal or instead of a meal, trying to forget what she'd lost, I think. Gamisis took her clothes and sold them after Mother died, keeping the money to buy me food, she said. Another lie no doubt. I certainly had no way to pay for a priest to recite blessings. I think Mother was buried in the town's common cemetery. So her ka has to wander endlessly, denied the Afterlife."

"I'll swear you another oath, when this is all over and we're free from our obligations to Egypt's defense, we'll journey to the town where you lost your mother. We'll find the temple of Renenutet or Horus or both and have the full Book of the Dead chanted in her name," Kamin said.

Nima regarded him with troubled eyes. "But Book of the Dead ceremonies cost much deben. I can't let you spend such a large amount on my mother's behalf."

He laughed. "The nomarch will pay. He's going to be extremely grateful to us for our services rendered. I keep telling you."

Exhaling a little puff of air, she shook her head. "All right, I believe you. For now."

Rising, Kamin walked over to the circle of ashes, stirring them with the toe of his sandal. "I'm sorry, but the bead dissolved in the flames."

Nima rubbed her wrist. "I'll miss it, but my mother said the whole reason I had the bead was to protect me. And now we've used up the amulet's power."

Kamin gazed at the ashes one more time, and a glint of light caught his eye. Reaching down, he pulled a single golden bead from the blackened circle. Holding it up to examine the carving, he blew gently and was rewarded by soot falling away from the bead's gleaming surface. Kamin saw the bauble was hollow, filigreed, carved as a nest of snakes sinuously curving around each other. It made him dizzy trying to figure out where one snake began and the next ended. "I think the goddess left you a replacement gift."

He brought the bead over to Nima, balanced in his palm.

"How beautiful!" Plucking the golden treasure from his hand, she held it to the sunlight. "But why would Renenutet leave this for me?"

"No one can pretend to understand the intent of the Great Ones," Kamin said. "She must feel you have need of it."

"A sobering thought. Maybe I shouldn't accept it." Nima frowned, eyebrows drawn together in a vee, her forehead wrinkled.

"Do you really think you have a choice?" he said softly. "Serious business, refusing a gift from the gods."

Ripping a thin strip from the hem of her already tattered skirt, Nima threaded it through the filigree of the bead before tying the length off to become a bracelet.

Studying her blotchy face, Kamin left well enough alone. "We'd better go or Renenutet and the servant of Horus will have killed all those hyenas for nothing."

When he lifted her from the sheltering rock formation, Nima tried to put her weight on the injured ankle and cried out, leaning heavily on him so as not to fall. She refused his offer to carry her, so he fashioned a staff of sorts from his bow, and she limped along next to him as they worked their way through the dead hyena pack, avoiding the black viscous gore pooled all over the sand.

After studying the map fragment briefly, Kamin pointed in the direction he'd decided to go. "I think we can find the track Ptahnetamun told me about if we go a bit north." Shielding his eyes with one hand, Kamin studied the sky. "Unless the falcon shows up to guide us otherwise."

Swirling just above the ground at ankle level, a small breeze blew off and on for the next hour, wiping away their tracks as they trudged.

CHAPTER EIGHT

Excruciatingly slow was the best pace she could manage. The first time they stopped to rest and drink water, she begged him to leave her.

"We've made such a pitiful amount of progress." Rubbing her foot, Nima tried to adjust the clumsy bandage. "You can go so much faster on your own."

"I'm not going to abandon you, so stop suggesting it," he said, a vein throbbing in his temple and eyes flashing angrily. "What kind of man do you think I am?"

"A sensible one," she answered, not cowed by his wrath. "Either Amarkash will catch up to us easily now or at best I'll slow you down so much, your news about their planned attacks won't reach the nomarch in time. You have to go on without me."

"Well, I won't, so you can stop bringing the idea up. I won't desert you." His touch gentle despite his angry tones, he handed her the bow and helped her rise from the rock where she'd perched.

Feeling honor-bound to dissuade him, Nima tried again. "You know Amarkash doesn't want me dead—"

Jaw clenched, Kamin stopped and faced her. "I will *not* sacrifice you nor allow you to sacrifice yourself *for* me, do you hear? I gave my oath to bring you to safety. I love you too much to leave you unprotected in the desert while I proceed alone. Don't ask me again."

In an uncomfortable silence they went on, Nima hobbling and trying not to cry from the worsening pain. Finally, exasperated, Kamin swept her into his arms and carried her, despite her protests. Late in the afternoon, they came upon a tiny oasis surrounding the remnants of a small, burned-out village. Leaving her hidden in the brush at the edge of the settlement, Kamin reconnoitered, sword in hand.

Soon enough, he returned, sheathing his weapon, face grim, mouth set and eyes bracketed with deep lines.

Reaching out to him anxiously, Nima rested one hand on his forearm. "What's wrong? What did you find?"

"The place is deserted. The Hyksos must have cleaned this small homestead out a long time ago from the looks of things. "

"But?" *What isn't he saying?* She tried to read his face. "There's something else, isn't there?"

He stood, gazing across the desert, arms at his side, fists clenched. "They left the bodies of those who were too old or too infirm to sell as slaves in a heap, on the other side of the oasis. " Bending over, he picked up a rock and hurled it as far away as he could. "May those bastards boil in the lake of fire!" Kamin turned to her, anguish and frustration in the set of his jaw, the glare in his hazel eyes. "These were simple people, a few families, minding their own business until Amarkash or some other jackal like him swooped in. Our people shouldn't be prey for those damned marauders."

Nima ached to go to him, hold him and offer comfort but was afraid her ankle wouldn't support her weight. Instead, she extended one hand. "You're doing the best you can for all of Egypt, Kamin. Pharaoh has to drive the would-be invaders out of Shield province and hold the borders to keep them from returning. Then women and children and their menfolk can live their lives in peace and safety. Your information will help achieve the ultimate victory. You told me so yourself, remember?"

He walked over and clasped her hand, bending to pick her up. "But I need to get my information to the nomarch in time to do something with it. Before any other settlement gets wiped out. Before the Hyksos are emboldened enough by their early successes to launch an attack on the cities. Before the province is lost."

Carrying her easily, he strode into the oasis. "We're staying here tonight. After I get you settled in one of the houses, I'll bury the poor villagers."

Nima inspected the damaged buildings they walked past. "Are we safe?"

"As safe as we'll be anywhere. Better than out in the open. The Great Ones will have to protect us tonight because you can't go any farther." He smiled, the expression hardly lightening the concern on his face. "We know the enemy soldiers are extremely reluctant to travel at night. At first light we'll be on our way again, staying ahead of Amarkash, don't worry. Your foot will be better in the morning, you'll see."

He's trying so hard to be positive for me. Heart aching, Nima averted her eyes from a wheeled child's toy, lying broken in the rubble. "What if they send another pack of those—those beasts after us? Or something worse?"

He grunted, juggling her in his arms a bit as he stepped over some rubble. "Hard to imagine anything worse."

"We should say something over the graves, after you've finished. It's the least we can do." Nima laid her head on his shoulder, blinking back tears, thinking hard. "Do you remember any passages from the Book of the Dead? You keep such a library in your head, or so you boast."

Giving her a sideways glance as he worked his way carefully through the ruins toward the least-destroyed house, Kamin seemed amused, a slight grin on his lips. "I'm hardly a priest."

"Never attended a funeral service? Never heard any of the chants?" She was disbelieving.

"My father's, several years ago." His face tightened.

Wishing she could soothe away the obviously painful memory, she kissed his cheek, the stubble scratching her lips a bit. "I'm sorry. I shouldn't have brought it up."

"No, you're right." He shook his head. "These people were innocent victims of war, and we're going to shelter in their home tonight, so we owe them something."

"If we recite even one blessing from the Book for them, the abbreviated ritual might win their sacred kas a chance to be judged by Anubis, get them into the

Afterlife." Sighing at the memory of the underworld, Nima said, "We know how beautiful it is there."

Holding her close, he kissed the top of her head. "You're an exceptional woman. The gods blessed me the day they sent you into my path."

"Oh, the day you were captured and beaten half to death?" Despite her teasing tone, she was pleased, warmed by his praise.

"Worth it, to find you." He sounded serious. Then he changed the subject. "I bagged a couple of rabbits while I was exploring the far side of this oasis. I'll clean them—"

Relieved to have a useful task she could perform while seated, Nima volunteered eagerly. "I'll be happy to sit and do the cooking. We can have a fire?"

"A small one," he said. "There's a good supply of clean-burning dung next to the hut I've picked for tonight, so a cooking fire shouldn't generate much smoke. I think Amarkash was counting on those hellhounds to track us and keep us cornered till we could be recaptured. Such spells take huge amounts of power, so the priest won't be able to work another one for a few days. And we didn't leave much in the way of tracks, thanks to the wind. Horus must have asked the Great One Shu to send the breeze our way."

"But the Hyksos will come after us eventually. Amarkash isn't giving up." Thinking back to her time as his captive, Nima knew she spoke the truth.

"The fact they exercised their god's power shows how much they want to get their hands on us," Kamin said, not disagreeing with her assessment.

He settled her inside a small, partially burned house, whose main amenity was an intact roof. After building a minuscule fire in the fire pit, he sat next to her, preparing the rabbit carcasses to be cooked. She unwrapped her foot, sucking in her breath as the fading sunlight streaming through the broken walls revealed ugly green and purple bruises bracketing gashes where the creature's teeth had savaged her.

"The wound is healing, definitely less angry red than before." Kamin leaned closer to check her injuries before resuming his food preparation. "How does your foot feel?"

Tracing the edge of the swollen area with her fingertip, she frowned. "About the same—aching. But not as damaged as when we first stopped on the rocks. And those scary black streaks under the skin are all gone."

"The kiss of Renenutet must have counteracted the poison in the wound. I was worried you'd lose the foot, to tell you the truth." Setting one last chunk of neatly trimmed meat for the stew on top of the pyramid he'd built, Kamin rinsed gristle and juices from his knife in a small bowl. "Thank the gods the priest who cast the spell was clumsy."

Nima bathed her ankle with the water he'd brought her in another salvaged basin. "I'd like to dance for Renenutet one day, to give proper thanks, you know?" Wincing, she lifted her dripping foot out of the shallow bowl and patted it dry. "Do you think the Great One would allow such a thing?"

"I don't know why not. A goddess should be pleased to have one of your skill perform for her."

"I'm not trained properly," Nima demurred.

"You'd be dancing from your heart, not stepping by rote through your training." Fetching more clean water from the well, he poured it into the stew pot, splashing a bit on the dirt floor of the house they'd commandeered for the night.

"I should see what herbs are in the gardens behind this house to season the stew, add sustenance. If there were to be aloe, I could make a poultice, and my ankle would heal faster," she said.

"Good idea. We can go harvest after you get the rabbit stew simmering on the fire." He shook his finger at her. "But no unusual spices in this kettle!"

She laughed. "Nothing but the basics, I promise, since there are no Hyksos to join us at dinner this time."

"Thank the gods." He searched through the piles of rubble in the one-room dwelling. "Will you be all right by yourself while I take care of the grim task awaiting me?"

Inclining her head slightly, Nima sighed. "Come get me when you're ready to chant, and I'll act as official mourner for these poor people."

He squeezed her hand and ducked out the door.

Stirring the stew lazily, Nima sat lost in thought, shifting occasionally, trying to find a more comfortable position for her foot. A feeling she was being watched gradually crept over her, making the skin between her shoulder blades itch and goose bumps rise along her arms. Turning her head, she let out a small scream.

Perched on the windowsill was an oversize gray and black falcon, staring at her with unblinking eyes.

One hand at her throat, ladle raised defensively in the other, Nima got to her knees, facing the bird. *Horus, this must be Horus.* But why would he seek her out? Kamin was sworn to his service, not she.

Spreading impressive wings, the falcon glided silently from the window, banking around her and landing beside the fire. Folding his wings again, the feathers on his back smoothing, the bird tilted his head.

Deciding to speak first rather than sit and cower, Nima said, "What is your wish, Great One?"

"You delay my warrior's progress."

The voice was deep, filling the small house, echoing off the damaged walls. Nima rocked back on her heels, ignoring the flash of pain from her wound. "I've tried to argue with him, make him leave me behind so he can reach help faster. He won't listen. He's sworn to protect me, and he's a man of honor." Pride in Kamin was a small glow of warmth against the chill of terror gripping her in the god's presence. She didn't know whether to be glad or sorry Horus was remaining in the bird form, rather than showing himself in all his glory. At easily ten times the size of a normal falcon, the bird was intimidating enough.

"His oaths to me and to Pharaoh, his duty to Egypt, come first before protecting you, woman." Horus sidled closer, cruel talons digging into the sandy floor.

Nima's thoughts whirled, and her tongue felt thick, paralyzed by her fear. *Is the god going to attack me?* She forced a few words to emerge. "I'm a loyal subject of Pharaoh, too, Great One."

"Loyalty is not enough. Action is required—*you* must be removed from the game board so my warrior can accomplish his task before all is lost." Horus folded his wings, preening a bit as he did so.

He's going to kill me. Nima's heart stuttered, and vertigo made her dizzy. Faster than she could blink, the falcon pecked at the golden bead on her wrist, tapping it with stinging force before he recoiled and back-winged in a flurry of feathers. She almost missed what the god said next.

"It seems Renenutet still acknowledges a connection to your fate. Not an insurmountable obstacle to one such as I, but her influence must be duly considered."

"You and she fought the Hyksos black magic together, back at the rock plateau," Nima reminded him, rubbing the red mark on her arm where his massive beak had struck. The golden bead seemed unharmed on its makeshift string bracelet.

Horus sat blinking for a long moment. Nima felt it was almost as if he was listening to someone else, although the tiny ruin of a house was utterly silent, aside from the crackling of the fire and her rapid breathing.

After flying to sit on top of a pile of rubble, the falcon puffed his chest feathers and spoke. "The enemies of Egypt would be satisfied to recapture you alone."

"Give myself up to them again? After all I went through—all *we've* gone through—to escape their net?" Taking a deep breath, Nima shut her eyes for a minute, unable to believe what Horus was suggesting. *Throw myself to the mercy of the Hyksos or die here?* Shaking her head, she stared at the falcon. "Kamin would follow me, as he's sworn to do, and either we'd both be taken prisoner again, or executed."

Rising to his full height, eyes gleaming uncannily in the shadows, the bird flared mighty wings for a moment. "Trust me to direct his steps once you are gone."

"Can you heal my ankle?" Nima asked the most logical thing first, hoping against hope. "Then we can proceed to safety together."

Apparently, her request caught him by surprise. Blinking, feathers rippling along his spine as if there was a breeze, Horus opened his beak in a hiss before answering. "I'm no healer, woman. I deal death to the enemies of Egypt. Look to others for the balm of healing."

"All right, then." She'd had scant hope the Great One would take pity on her and mend her foot. Now to keep him from freeing Kamin from distractions by sending her to the Afterlife permanently. "I've no intention to offend, but I've a mundane request—can you bring me something from the garden?"

*****

Later, as the orange sun touched the clouds at the horizon in a flare of purples and reds, Kamin returned to the hut after taking a makeshift bath outside by the well. She could hear him splashing, and his hair was wet when he re-entered the hut. Nima and Horus had concluded their business long before, after which the Great One had taken his leave, and she didn't mention the god's visit.

When he'd cleaned up as best he could, Kamin carried her to the other side of the village, where they stood side by side next to the freshly mounded soil. Weaving together excerpts from various portions of the Book of the Dead, he chanted in a rich baritone, requesting the Great Ones who ruled the Afterlife to allow the poor souls of the nameless village free passage to the joys of the *duat*. Leaning on him, Nima felt a sensation of peace come over her as he uttered the sacred words. Surely, even though the two of them had no ability to perform all the complicated rituals called for, the gods would accept what had been done as enough.

When Kamin completed his prayers, he nodded to her, and she cast a handful of wildflowers on the grave, saying from the heart as she did so, "May you each ride in the boat of Ra the Sun and be received graciously in the court of Osiris the king, to find the joy and peace torn from you in life. May your names be known to the gods for all time as true Egyptians."

Far out in the desert, a falcon shrieked a challenge as thunder rolled. Losing her balance, Nima startled, pulse pounding. Kamin caught her in his arms.

"I hope someone will do us this much honor when we're departed from the earth," Nima said as Kamin picked her up to carry her to their temporary refuge.

"I wish it hadn't been necessary," he answered. "I wish the Hyksos were gone from these lands and Nat-re-Akhte could rule our people in peace."

Twining her arms around his neck, leaning as close as she could get, Nima said, "Surely the map and other information you carry will affect the balance of power in this province, tilt the scales for Egypt."

"We'll see. I've worked up an appetite now, carrying you," he teased. "Will the stew be done soon?"

She pushed at his shoulder, her small fist making no impression on his well-sculpted muscles. "I weigh next to nothing, and you know it, soldier. But, yes, I think we could eat."

He had two bowls of her delicious rabbit stew, augmented with vegetables they'd harvested in the abandoned gardens. Although he urged her to eat, Nima dined sparingly. As night fell, they curled up together beside the fire in the ruins of the small house, Kamin holding her close, until she was sure he had fallen asleep, despite his expressed intention to remain alert and on guard through the night. Nima waited until his breathing evened out, and he was deeply lost in slumber before wriggling from his arms. *Thank goodness the garden held both the herbs to drug him into sleep and the ones I needed to stay unaffected.* She took another pinch of the latter for good measure now, swallowing the powdered leaves with water from the pitcher. Tenderly, she covered him with his cloak, dropping a kiss on his cheek. Dousing the fire so no passing enemies would see it and investigate, she retrieved the cane she'd created for herself after the encounter with Horus. Using the cane she'd fashioned from a broken table leg, she hobbled to the doorway.

Pausing for one last look at her lover, Nima wiped away a tear. *I wish I could write, wish I could leave him a note, something to beg his forgiveness.* "Please don't hate me, Kamin, no matter what Horus chooses to tell you." Resolutely, she walked into the moonlight and made her way into the desert, painfully retracing the route they had taken.

CHAPTER NINE

Barely conscious, Nima walked aimlessly, limping through the hot sands. She traveled to the west. *Or maybe I'm going in circles.* She'd had no water since the morning and had lost the cane at some point along the way. Her foot throbbed with every step, and her back ached dully, thrown out of kilter by the need to limp. Hearing the rumble of chariots and shouting behind her, she sank to the ground, arms resting on her knees, head down. Her heart pounded in her chest, but even stark terror failed to energize her enough to fight or flee.

The Hyksos chariots swept to a halt in a rough circle with her at the center, dust swirling into the air, making her cough. Amarkash jumped from the nearest vehicle and strode over to her, grabbing her hair with enough force to make her head ache. "Egyptian bitch, you've led us a long chase." He slapped her across the face, and she fell on her side, curling into a ball.

"Water," she begged through cracked lips. "Please."

Two soldiers yanked her to her feet, and a cry of pure agony ripped from her throat as the men tried to make her walk.

"I can't put any weight on my foot. Your hellhounds bit me." She wept, clinging to the nearest warrior's greasy leather breastplate, keeping the toes of her right foot from touching the ground.

Amarkash came closer, gesturing to his men. "Let her sit. Unwrap her foot."

As the ugly bruises and bite marks were revealed, he hissed through his teeth, spinning on his heel to confront a man near the chariots. "Priest! Your creatures weren't supposed to damage her."

Drinking casually from a bulging water skin, a pudgy celebrant of Qemtusheb strolled to join Nima and the captain. He wiped his mouth and replaced the stopper, smiling as Nima watched his every move, licking her painfully cracked lips. He waggled the container in her direction. "You want water, don't you? Well, perhaps in a moment or two, if you behave."

"If you tell us what we want to know," Amarkash amended. Leaning over, he grabbed her chin, forcing Nima to look up at him. "Where's your lover? What happened to the soldier?"

"He left me. I couldn't keep up with him after your beasts savaged my foot. He said I was a useless burden. He took all the water we'd gotten from the caravan," she said sullenly.

"More likely he tired of your scrawny body." Amarkash rested his hands on his hips and stared at the sky for a long moment while Nima waited. "Oh, all right, give her something to drink. But not too much."

Grabbing at the water skin a soldier handed her, Nima tried not to gulp, lest drinking too fast make her ill.

"Can you heal her foot?" Amarkash demanded of the priest while she sipped the water.

"Let me see." Instinctively, she inched away when he knelt beside her. He smelled of some powerful spice, with an underlying hint of coppery blood. Ragged beard and jagged yellow teeth completed the picture. Despite the heat of the day, his fleshy hands were cold as he unwound the bandages and poked and probed her ankle. Nima clenched her teeth, nails digging into her palms at the pain he so casually inflicted. After a moment, he gestured to Amarkash to come closer. "This is most unusual."

The captain flicked his whip against his leg impatiently. "What?"

"Observe what happens when I touch her." The priest laid his hand on her calf. His handprint showed black for a moment on her skin, then flared red and disappeared.

"Stop touching me," Nima said, swatting at his hand. "The pressure on my skin hurts."

"She has power of some sort." The priest sounded excited. "She would make an excellent sacrifice. Kill a vessel of power like this girl, and Qemtusheb is drawn to appear."

"I don't know what you're talking about. I'm a dancer," Nima protested, pulse racing in fear. All Egypt knew the Hyksos practiced human sacrifice to their god. A person's ka was destroyed in the process, never to know the Afterlife, no matter how many prayers were offered later.

"You hope you're still a dancer," Amarkash retorted coldly. "General Nebuchazz will have no use for a lame performer. He won't even want to bed you—he can't abide physical flaws."

Rubbing his hands on the back of his red and black-striped robes, the priest stood. "I can't heal the wound. Even though the creatures I summoned caused the damage, the power in her body interferes with mine. She'll have to heal herself, if it can be done at all."

"Of course I'll heal," Nima said. "It takes time."

Amarkash coiled the whip, and she cringed. Terror made her weakened body tremble. Nausea threatened to overwhelm her.

"We don't have time." Amarkash spat and wiped his mouth on his sleeve. "We've been chasing you all over this damned desert for days. General Nebuchazz wanted you to dance for him on our major feast day, which falls in less than a week." Releasing his grip on Nima, the captain frowned at the priest. "Consider carefully whether you can heal her or not." He held up a hand as the priest tried to protest. "All I'm saying is, if Nebuchazz ever finds out you could have healed her and didn't, because you wanted her as a blood sacrifice, he'll exact vengeance. So think carefully what spells you might know for repairing a damaged ankle." He signaled to the soldiers. "Bring her to my chariot. Now we've found the general's wayward treasure, we can proceed to the fortress. No more time wasted."

They don't even want Kamin. The officer who had captured him must not have told the other Hyksos Kamin was a spy. So giving myself up means he'll be able to escape. Nima swallowed hard against the bile rising in her throat as a burly soldier carried her over his shoulder to the waiting chariot, one callused hand caressing her bottom through the dress. Ignoring her whimpers of pain, Amarkash bound her wrists roughly behind her and hobbled her ankles. "I'm taking no chances with you. I'll not lose you again. And you won't be cooking for us. You may sit in my chariot, since you can't stand on your damaged ankle." Shoving her in front of him, he picked up the reins and whip and set his horses into motion.

Trying not to give in to her tears, Nima leaned against the side of the jolting vehicle as they raced deeper into the desert toward the distant, purple mountain range.

*****

Groggily, Kamin rolled over and sat up, throwing the tangled cloak aside. His head felt stuffed with cotton and ached abominably at the same time. Vision blurry, he rubbed his eyes. "Nima?" *It's too quiet.* He lurched to his feet, grabbing at the wall of the ramshackle hut to keep his balance. After the vertigo passed, he tried opening his eyes again and surveyed the shack. *Her cloak is missing. Wings of Horus, what has she done?*

His stomach cramped, and he barely made it outside the building in a stumbling run before he threw up all he had eaten. *Her cursed herbs—she did use them on me. She must have stirred them in my bowl of stew when I wasn't paying attention.* But it wasn't anger coursing through his body to clear the drug-induced fog; rather, the icy grip of sheer terror closed around his heart. *How long has she been gone? How much of a head start does she have on me? Little fool, sacrificing herself to draw the Hyksos away from my trail! I told her I wouldn't accept such a sacrifice.*

Shuffling into the house, he grabbed his weapons and the supplies she'd left him, and headed for the edge of the tiny oasis, regaining more and more of his coordination by the minute. Hand shading his eyes, he stepped out from under the palm trees onto the sands, scanning the ground for any telltale tracks.

The falcon swooped at him, screaming.

Kamin ducked and covered his face from the attack, retreating. Drawing his sword to fend off anymore aggression from the bird, he raised his shield and headed for the footprints.

Gliding right over his head, the bird landed directly in front of him, growing to man size in the blink of an eye, black and gray-banded wings flared to impede his progress.

"I can't allow her to be retaken," he said to the bird, veering off to the left to work his way beyond the obstacle. "I love her."

Green light flared, temporarily blinding him. As Kamin's vision returned, the bird transformed into a warrior, standing taller than he, holding a golden shield and a gleaming sword throwing off the rays of the desert sun. The god's finely pleated kilt was white and gold, and on his head he wore the towering red and white crown. A stylized hawk pectoral in turquoise, gold and coral stretched across his impressively muscled, bare chest, the colors echoed in his gem-studded belt. For a moment after taking human form, the pupils of Horus's eyes remained in their godly guise—one a diamond sun casting rainbows and the other a silver moon. "What of the oaths you swore, to me and to Nat-re-Akhte, your Pharaoh?" Glaring at Kamin, blinking his eyes back to a more normal black, Horus pointed the sword at his chest. "Do you love her more than Egypt? Is her life worth more than the Black Lands themselves?"

Shield in front of him, Kamin knelt on one knee, sword held upright. *My heart wants to shout yes, Nima's life is worth any price to me. Better choose my words carefully.* "With all due respect, Great One, Nima doesn't deserve to die to save me. She can't have gone far yet, so I can catch up to her. She's injured. She thinks she'd slow me down too much—"

"And she's right." Horus raised one hand, closing his fist as he did so, and the tracks dissolved as if blown away by a faint breeze. "Think, warrior, with your head, not your heart." Echoes of his words rumbled across the dunes like distant thunder. "There is this one chance to strike a mighty blow at those who threaten Egypt. If the Hyksos' secret base is destroyed, the setback will repel the evil their god seeks to impose on Egypt. You alone have the information to guide the nomarch's army to the hidden fortress. You alone hold the key to cutting off the head of the serpent, their most crafty general." Horus watched him closely, head forward and tilted as the falcon might do when evaluating prey. "What is the life of one girl against the loss of an entire province of Egypt?"

Kamin could hardly think for the ache in his heart. He forced a deep breath of the hot desert air into his lungs. *Egypt or Nima? I know what I want to choose, but I also know my duty. I must try another tack with the Great One.* "Her life matters more to me than my own."

Horus nodded. "Acknowledged, warrior, but loss of this nome will be a serious crack in your country's defenses. Not lightly did the ancients name this province as Shield of Egypt."

Pain gnawing at his gut, Kamin slowly shook his head. "Nima would be the first to agree, obviously, since she's trying to draw Amarkash away from me and the information I carry." He stared longingly at the patch of sand where Nima's footprints had been before Horus had obliterated them. Rolling his shoulders and straightening his spine, Kamin stood, gazing straight into the god's mesmerizing eyes. "I hear and obey your command, Great One—"

"As a soldier should do."

"But I ask a boon in return."

Horus met the challenge with a blink, his pupils reverting to the sun and the moon, casting rainbows and silvery illumination around them both until Kamin was dizzy. Thunder rumbled in the distance, and green light flashed in the darkened sky. The Great One grew even taller. "What is it you ask? Do you wish me to guarantee she'll be waiting for you in the Afterlife?"

Remaining resolute, even as the god's voice buffeted him like wind gusts, Kamin shook his head. *I dream of having Nima in* this *life*. "I want the chance to rescue her. I want the opportunity to lead the army to the enemy's fortress in time to accomplish both goals, Egypt's and my own."

"A nicely balanced supplication." Horus considered, head tipped sideways again, eyes going black. "The enemy has created a space wherein their god reigns supreme. I can't reach into their citadel and pluck her out."

Looking away, Kamin studied the desert around them. *Something has to be possible, even with Qemtusheb's influence causing problems. She and I struggled so hard.* "Great One, can you delay the Hyksos on their way to the compound? Send sandstorms, broken chariots, lame horses, anything to give me time?" Hope warmed his heart as he rattled off the suggestions. "My Nima is clever—she can probably thwart their plans for her somewhat even after she arrives at their stronghold, but I'm going to need a fatter margin of days to get the army mobilized and on the move."

Throwing back his head, the god laughed, sand swirling away from him in giant vortexes at the sound. "A cosmic game of senet! Play tricks on our adversaries as they cross the open desert I can, and will do, warrior. I swear upon the scales of truth overseen by my sister Ma'at, I'll delay the enemy on their journey through the Red Lands." Raising the sword, Horus pointed at the horizon to the east. "Now get *you* gone to Tentaris."

*****

After many long, frustrating days on the trail, the Hyksos column finally straggled through the gates of the massive fortress. Nima's ankle was a bit improved today, and she stood in the chariot next to Amarkash as he led his troops inside. The huge wooden gates slammed shut behind the stragglers of their group. Glancing around the courtyard, Nima did a quick count of the fleet of waiting chariots parked alongside the walls. She eyed the stacks of swords, maces, bows and arrows.

"You stockpile the tools of war," she said, trying to ignore the sinking feeling in the pit of her stomach. *They must have a massive army to need so many weapons.*

"We've been busy, Egyptian. While your pharaoh takes his time to the north, ensuring his secure seat on the throne, my people scout this province, make our plans, set our spies in place. Soon, very soon, we'll be marching from this forsaken mountain and grabbing victory. We only await the blessing of our god at the festival to launch the offensive. He's been most favorable to our efforts so far. This stronghold is protected by his powers. None of your inferior Egyptian gods can enter or even spy upon us." Amarkash grabbed her by the ropes on her wrists. "You're worrying about the wrong subjects, girl. We're going to see General Nebuchazz now. He's much more your concern than strategies and battles."

Nima didn't offer any resistance as he pulled her from the chariot. Being in the actual citadel after so many days of trying to avoid that very destination weighed on her like a stone in the gut. The place was ominous and dark, permeated by an intense spicy scent, giving her a dull headache. The idea the Hyksos planned to launch their offensive so soon circled around in her mind like a dust devil. Could Kamin get the nomarch's army ready for such an onslaught in time? *Can I do anything to delay their plans?* Nima laughed ruefully under her breath. She was hardly in a position to take action on Egypt's behalf.

Amarkash carried her across the courtyard, into the cool darkness of the central building, the priest pacing alongside. The captain strode along as if Nima's weight was nothing. The halls were crowded with soldiers, leering at her as they pressed themselves against the walls to clear a path. She heard unmistakably lascivious comments, even if she didn't understand the exact words. Holding her head as high as she could, Nima avoided eye contact.

I hope you got away safely, Kamin, got to the nomarch with your information by now. Matters are at a more dangerous pass than we thought. She hated Amarkash touching her body. His long, bony fingers dug into her flesh, making her skin crawl. Nima tried to hold herself rigidly away from contact with him as much as possible, even as he grinned and hugged her closer.

Her captor carried her into an antechamber, guarded by tall, well-muscled warriors, showing more precision and discipline than Nima had seen displayed by any of the army before, even by Amarkash himself. The officer of the watch sent a man to inform the general of their arrival. Setting Nima on her feet while they waited, Amarkash kept his proprietary hold on her elbow with one hand, while brushing the dust off his kilt with the other. The sentry reappeared in the doorway shortly, reporting the general would see the new arrivals at once. Beckoning them to follow, the officer marched toward the next chamber. Amarkash gestured for Nima to precede him.

"You walk on your own two feet now, dancer, and make the best of it you can." He leaned close. "General Nebuchazz is not merciful."

She limped along next to him.

The renowned general was a small man, barely taller than she, intense, with a shaven head, a pointed black beard, and intensely frowning eyes. She trembled to find she recognized him. *I remember him. He made me uneasy when I danced at the Blue Lotus inn. And then he showed up again a few days later at the next place we performed.*

Seated behind a table full of maps and papyrus scrolls, Nebuchazz shot one dismissive glance at her, did a slower double-take, raising one bushy eyebrow, and frowned.

He slammed his fist on the table, making the papers and the ink stand jump. Nima flinched. When the general spoke, his voice was low and deliberate. "By the lake of fire, what joke is this, Amarkash?"

"I bring you the dancer, as ordered, sir." Amarkash's face was expressionless, his voice bland, but the muscle twitching in his cheek close to his right eye betrayed tension.

Pushing the maps aside with a careless gesture, Nebuchazz left his chair to stalk Nima. Instinctively, she retreated, mesmerized by the intense expression on his face, raising her bound hands in a futile attempt to ward him off. Like a crocodile, he made a sudden lunge to grab her by one shoulder. Studying her face from just inches away, his breath smelling of garlic and spoiled meat, he rubbed a fading bruise on her cheek with his fingertip. "Much the worse for the trip, apparently. I told you she was to be untouched." He shoved Nima away from him as if expecting Amarkash to catch her. Ankle buckling under the force of his violent rejection, she crumpled to the floor with a cry.

The general stood over her with hands on his hips, eyebrows rising practically to his bald pate. He nudged her hip with one sandaled foot. "And she's injured as well?"

"The ankle is healing—" Nima said, massaging the joint awkwardly.

Grabbing her tangled hair, Nebuchazz yanked her to her knees. "If I desire to hear your voice, I'll command it. Best not to speak again uninvited, or I might decide to cut out your pretty pink tongue, no matter how talented." For the second time, he shoved her, and Nima bit her lip not to moan as she sank to the cold stone floor. Above her head, the general said, "What happened to her? Why is she no longer the beautiful flower I remember, the woman I sent your patrol to fetch for me?"

"She escaped with an Egyptian soldier our other patrol had captured," Amarkash reported crisply. "Somehow, the pair killed the soldiers I sent after them, eluding capture for over a week. After I located her, we were delayed on our journey here by a series of mishaps."

"Mishaps?" Nebuchazz tilted his head. "Explain yourself."

"Sandstorms blocked my column's progress twice, and then we had a series of broken chariot wheels." Amarkash ticked off the disasters on his fingers. "I had to sit and wait while my patrols went on foot to find an oasis with trees suitable for mending the wheels. I lost two teams of horses to—"

Nebuchazz held up one hand, closing his fingers into a fist.

Biting his lip until he drew a bead of bright red blood, Amarkash shut up.

"I assume the soldier is dead," the general said. It was not phrased as a question.

No one contradicted him, Nima least of all. *You never would have caught Kamin.* Nima comforted herself, a little flame of warmth in her mind and heart. *I was his weakness, and I solved the problem for him.*

Drumming his fingers on the edge of the table, the general asked, "You fail to address my pertinent question—how was she injured?"

Stabbing a finger in the priest's direction, Amarkash deflected the general's ire away from himself. "This one unleashed the devil dogs of Qemtusheb on her."

"You did what?" Turning on his heel, Nebuchazz stalked toward the priest, who scuttled sideways, alarm on his suddenly pale face. One of the guards prevented his exit from the room, using his spear to trap the man in a corner.

Scooting herself farther away from the ugly and dangerous drama, Nima grabbed the corner of the table, pulling herself shakily to her feet.

The priest raised his hands as if to ward off the general. "I wanted to shorten the time we were spending chasing her all over the desert. To—to bring her to you sooner. The black magic beasts—they were only supposed to track her, my lord, not touch her. She has power of her own and must have altered my spell."

All eyes in the room turned to her. The general tilted his head, fingering his belt knife and stroking his beard. "Well, what say you to this accusation, woman?"

Finding her voice, Nima said, "I'm a dancer from the border towns, not some priestess or sorceress with dark powers." She extended her right leg like a heron might, balancing on her good side while hanging on to the table for dear life. "See what the creatures did to my foot?"

Nebuchazz spared a rapid glance in the direction of her lower limbs. Then in between one breath and another, he took his dagger from his belt and stabbed the priest through the heart.

Nima's throat closed in terror. She couldn't even scream. Seeking anything she could use as a weapon to make a fight of it if the general came in her direction, she eyed the writing utensils on the table.

"Take this offal out of my office," Nebuchazz said to no one in particular, yanking his knife free and stepping away from the corpse of the man he'd summarily executed.

Two soldiers leaped to do his bidding, dragging the unfortunate priest's body out by the heels, a long smear of blood left behind on the stone floor.

Stoically, Amarkash watched as a servant hurried in and wiped the floor with water and rags. "And the girl, sir?"

Cleaning his knife, Nebuchazz eyed Nima dispassionately, his face calm. "The festival is approaching rapidly, but I'll not insult the god by having a limping dancer." Walking to Nima, he circled her waist with his free arm and drew her close, resting the tip of the dagger in the hollow of her throat. "Dance for me in two days time as you did at the Egyptian taverns, with passion to stir my loins," he said, "I'll spare your life, make you my personal slave. I can be quite generous. If you fail to please, I'll sell you to the highest bidder on the spot. Do I make myself clear?"

She nodded, not trusting herself to speak. *And I was refusing to dance for lecherous Egyptian nobles—they're nothing compared to this man's arrogance. He's danger personified.*

As abruptly as he'd seized her, Nebuchazz let her go. "So, if you are a woman of power, as the priest claimed, turn your magic on yourself." Seating himself behind the desk again, he picked up a tablet, scanning the symbols, openly dismissing Nima and Amarkash. Not looking up again, he issued crisp orders. "Lock her in a cell but ensure she's well treated, well fed. Have her bathed, dressed in clean clothing. I want the physician to treat her ankle twice each day."

"As you command, sir." Amarkash saluted and picked her up, foiling her efforts to limp out of the room on her own.

When he'd carried her into the hall, the captain put his lips next to her ear, holding her tightly as she tried to wriggle away. "I might buy you myself. There's no way you're going to be able to dance for Nebuchazz, is there?"

"I don't know," Nima lied. *I'll be lucky if I can hobble across the room in two days, much less dance.*

His hand moving to close painfully on her breast, thumb caressing her nipple through the dress, Amarkash whispered, "I'll enjoy stripping you naked, wrapping you in ropes again, playing games with no limits this time, when you're mine, not his."

She was actually glad when they headed down a dank, dead-end corridor lined with heavy wooden doors, each with one small, barred window in the center. Carrying her into the last cell, the captain deposited her on a cot. "Servants will bring you what the general has authorized, and I'm sure the doctor will attend you shortly. Likely we'll not meet again until your attempt to dance in two days. And then, if Nebuchazz lets you live, I'll buy you." He winked suggestively as she glared at him. Drawing his knife, he sliced the cords on her wrists and left the cell. A grim-faced soldier closed the door, and Nima heard heavy bolts being shot home a moment later.

She contemplated the dank interior of the cell. *At least it's clean, and I don't see any vermin. Bugs, yes, rats, no. Two days. I have two days to live.* Extending her leg, she tried to point the toes on her injured foot, flexing and stretching the tendons, ignoring the pain until it made her nauseated. *I'm not going to be able to dance. I don't even want to dance.* Shuddering, she flicked a scurrying, many-legged insect away from her.

The cell door opened again, and several servants entered, carrying clothing and food as ordered by Nebuchazz. By their facial tattoos, the women were from some southern tribe and didn't speak any language known to Nima but smiled at her shyly, relieving the tension somewhat. Watching avidly, the guard stood in the doorway as the two serving girls helped her disrobe and conduct an awkward bath. Nima burned with embarrassment and anger, but the maids tried to keep themselves between the guard and her, holding up towels and clothing to obscure his view.

The doctor arrived before she was quite dressed. Tall, thin, garbed in the standard Hyksos brown and gray, he tolerated no nonsense. "I want no audience here. If you aren't my patient, get out," he said, pointing at the servant girls. Then he studied Nima. "You, sit." He made a shooing motion to the guard, still leaning insolently against the open door. "You, go. I'll call you if there's any need."

The man moved aside to let the two slaves pass, then stepped inside the cell. "But the prisoner—"

"Is a woman. She won't harm me. Will you?" He looked at Nima over his shoulder, eyebrows raised.

"No." She tried not to laugh sarcastically at the question. *I'm anxious to see if he can help me. The last thing I want to do right now is harm the doctor.*

He turned to the guard. "Well, then, there you have it, no danger to me. No one eavesdrops on a physician's consultation with his patient, even one who is a prisoner. Get *out*."

The guard scowled but stalked out, slamming the heavy door behind him aggressively.

The doctor laughed. "The soldiers hate taking orders from me, but no man wants to alienate the army's physician, lest they need my services someday." Walking to the bed, he set his wooden box of instruments and potions on the thin mattress.

"Thank you," Nima said through gritted teeth, hobbling to the bed and sitting as she had been ordered.

"There are few women in this forsaken place. Not many slaves are kept here when they can be sold for a profit. Going out on the raids, being allowed to rape and pillage, is a privilege accorded to only a few of the platoons stationed at this outpost. You're attracting a great deal of attention in the garrison." He knelt and took her ankle in firm but gentle hands, examining the gashes closely.

"I don't wish to be an object of attention." She flinched as he manipulated her ankle.

"Don't fidget, I need to assess the damage," he said unsympathetically, flexing the foot in the other direction. "Well, until you've danced for the general, no one will do more than leer at you. You might have to endure some furtive fondling from the charming fellow outside your door." He frowned. "But once you've failed Nebuchazz's test, you'll be fair game." Whistling, he released Nima and opened the top of his lacquered cedar box, sorting through the contents of the many drawers cunningly folded inside. "It's pleasant to have a professional challenge other than sword and arrow wounds."

"We both know I'm not going to be able to dance." Closing her eyes, Nima shook her head.

The doctor brought out a small pot of strong-smelling ointment. The odor immediately permeated the small cell. Gagging, Nima wrinkled her nose and put her hand over her mouth. "Horse liniment?"

"Yes." He slathered the smelly green cream on her foot and ankle. The ointment delivered soothing heat as he massaged it into her skin in small, circular motions, banishing the throbbing pain. "If liniment works for the general's favorite chariot horse, why not for the general's favorite dancer?"

Nima laughed, until she felt the mirth edging into tears. *I can't lose my self-control in this place.* Shuddering, she tried to quell her emotions as the doctor finished ministering to her with cold efficiency and packed his supplies away. He stood, evaluating her. "Do you want something to help you sleep, calm your nerves?"

"I doubt you have a potion strong enough to make me forget the threat of becoming Nebuchazz's personal slave." She curled her lip, tossing her head. "Despite his claim of being extremely *generous*, not an enticing future."

"Your other choices are worse," the doctor pointed out, handing her a small cup of green liquid with pieces of leaves and stems floating on top. "I'll examine you again in the morning, since the sun goes down already today. The liniment can't be applied too often or your skin will suffer." He nodded at the small table covered with plates and bowls of food and a pitcher of water. "I suggest you eat, perhaps try to sleep. You'll need your beauty intact to placate Nebuchazz." Strolling to the door, he pounded on it with his fist. "'Til the morning," he said over his shoulder.

The guard let the physician out, but paused to gaze at Nima's body for a long minute before slamming the door shut again.

She set the medicine on the table and listlessly examined the array of dishes— quail, a half-spoiled plum, two kinds of bread. None of it appealed to her. Breaking the fruit bowl on the stone floor, she kept the biggest, jagged shard as a deterrent, should the guard make a middle of the night visit. Shaking out the scratchy blanket the slaves had brought, she curled up on the cot, against the wall, forcing herself to blot out all thoughts except the ones having to do with Kamin, trying to comfort herself against the terrors of the night and the days to follow. She left the small oil lamp on the table burning. *I pray light can keep the nightmares at bay.*

CHAPTER TEN

The next day passed slowly. The doctor came twice, as ordered, slathering more of the strong-smelling liniment on her foot. She tried a few tentative dance steps when she was alone, humming a tune with an easy beat, but soon collapsed on the cot, near tears. *Even if I wanted to dance for Nebuchazz, I can't. My ankle is too weak.*

The slaves brought her dinner, and the guard lingered in the cell after the women left.

"What do you want?" Nima picked up a piece of flat bread and nibbled at it to hide her nervousness.

Eyes locked on her chest, he came closer, rubbing his hands. "I've told my friends in the barracks you won't be able to dance tomorrow. I've seen you practicing and weeping, through the bars." He jerked a finger over his shoulder.

"So?" Nima dropped the bread to the floor and backed away from the man's overwhelming odor of sweat and onions. "What is it to you? Or your friends?"

"We're pooling our money to buy you, to try to outbid the officers. I wanted to let you know, so you could think about ways to please your new masters." He reached out one hand, grabbing her by the elbow in an attempt to drag her closer. "There'll be ten of us, at least."

Slapping him hard enough to bruise her hand, Nima almost fell. The guard cursed as he crushed her in a forced embrace, the buckles on his leather breastplate digging painfully into her breasts. Laughing, he ran his hand over her body, lower and lower, until he was cupping her through the dress. "I'm thinking I should sample the wares a little, eh?"

"Let go of me, you inbred jackal." Nima slammed her head up into his chin and tried to whirl away, but her ankle betrayed her and she fell. In her hand she brandished his belt dagger, which she had grabbed. "Leave me alone, I warn you."

The guard circled her as she scooted to get her back to the wall, managing to stand up, holding the dagger at the ready.

A sharp voice brought them both to a halt. "What is the meaning of this?"

An officer Nima had never seen before stood in the doorway. Cheeks flushed, the guard saluted and stood at attention. "The prisoner is trying to escape, sir."

"You know it's death to lay a hand on her before the general releases his claim. You're a good man, corporal, if stupid, so I won't report your rash action. Retrieve your knife from the wench and lock her in." The man stood watching as Nima reluctantly handed back the dagger and the guard stalked out of the cell, slamming the door with enough force to set the small lamp flickering.

Limping to the bed, Nima lay down, curling up with her back to the door. Fingering the knotted cloth bracelet on her wrist, she sighed. *If only the officer hadn't come along, I could have stabbed that lout of a guard and gotten out of the cell. Just give me half a deben's worth of luck, and I'll be gone from this evil place.* She rolled the golden bead around the string with her fingers for a moment before drawing a deep breath and holding it, excited. Could she use this last gift from Renenutet to summon supernatural help? Nima frowned as she examined the bead more closely in the dim light. Amarkash had said this fortress was under some kind of all-encompassing spell from their god Qemtusheb. And who knows what kind of aid the snakes could give her in this situation anyway?

Rolling over onto her back, Nima stared at the dancing shadows the lamp cast on the ceiling. *If you only have one weapon, how foolish not to unleash it? I'm going to die tomorrow anyway since I can't dance for Nebuchazz. What if I could call the snakes and create some chaos? Some destruction? Some deaths?* Grinning, Nima sat up. *Anything I could do to delay the attack they're planning on Egypt buys time for*

Kamin and the nomarch's army. If not for myself, I should try to summon the snakes for his sake.

Curling up again, in case the lecherous guard was watching through the bars in the door's small window, Nima surreptitiously untied the knot holding the bead on the strings, catching the bauble in one hand as it rolled free on the scratchy blanket. Bringing it closer to her eyes in the dim light, she studied the filigree. The bead appeared to be five snakes, entwined. Slowly, trying to be noiseless, Nima uncoiled and slid off the bed, going to fetch the remnants of the flat bread from her dinner. Carrying the crumbly, moldy bread back to the bed, she set the golden bead in the center, as Kamin had done on the rocky plateau.

Now what? Blood, she needed a drop of blood. Nauseated, she scratched at her injured ankle for a moment, until a single drop of blood welled up. Using the string from the bracelet as a wick, Nima soaked up the ruby fluid and daubed the bead and the bread.

But what to say? Even Kamin had seemed to just speak his mind, not utter any preset incantation. Licking her lips, Nima whispered her most fervent desire. "Great One, I thank thee for this gift, and I beseech you to give life to the serpents, to help me escape tonight while inflicting damage on these enemies of Egypt."

She waited expectantly. Ten heartbeats, then ten more.

Nothing.

"More blood? Different words?" she said under her breath. "Oh, this is ridiculous. Perhaps the goddess truly only meant the bead to be a piece of jewelry, although why—"

Tiny gold and red sparks were flying into the air from the bead, disappearing into the gloom. She sat bolt upright, watching wide-eyed as the five tiny serpents untangled themselves from each other. Only a few inches long, they were too beautiful to be frightening, golden scales glinting as each slowly undulated across the blanket, ruby eyes glowing in the darkness of her cell. Reaching out in wonder, Nima let the closest snake crawl into her hand, exclaiming at the tickling sensation as the snake's belly rasped across her palm. The snake coiled for a moment, hood flared, wisp of an emerald tongue flicking in and out, tasting the air.

One of the others slithered across the bed, falling off the side. As Nima watched, still holding the first snake, the free-falling reptile winked out in a blaze of colorful sparks just as it hit the floor. Worried if she didn't move quickly, she'd lose them all, Nima got off the bed, hand closed around the snake she held. Its tongue touched her fingers in featherlight sensations. She grabbed her mug with her free hand, tossed the dregs on the floor and dropped the snake into it, going back to the bed to catch the others. A second snake was working its way down the wooden leg of the bed, and Nima managed to capture it by the tail just before it reached the floor, dropping her captive into the cup with its fellow. Yet even as she did so, a third snake disappeared in a soundless explosion of color. She was searching in the blanket for the fifth when a voice spoke from right behind her.

"Foolish girl, you squander the weapons I gave you."

Renenutet—for it was the snake goddess herself, in human form—reached past Nima's shoulder, holding out one hand. The remaining three snakes flew through the air to her like tiny arrows, wrapping themselves around her wrist to create a fabulous bracelet.

Heart pounding, Nima sank down on the bed.

Stroking the living bracelet as if to calm the snakes while frowning at Nima, the goddess said, "You can't call the snakes of Nebu merely to amuse yourself, girl."

You didn't exactly provide me a scroll of instructions with the gift. Nima bit her tongue as she left the bed to go to her knees before the Great One. "I'm grateful for your continued assistance, my lady."

The goddess reached out to stroke her hand through Nima's hair, patting her cheek as a mother might. "You are so like her, and she was my favorite."

"My mother?" Nima asked hesitantly.

"Yes. She was trained to my service from the day she could walk, would have been the high priestess over all my temples one day. She was like a daughter to me, the child of my heart. Until she let herself be distracted—" Renenutet frowned, withdrawing her hand, and the snakes on her wrist writhed, hissing.

"Distracted by my father." Nima closed her eyes for a moment, wishing for the thousandth time with a dull aching pain in her heart that her mother had told her more about the mysterious father she'd never met.

"You and I must both let the past go, child," Renenutet answered in a low voice.

The goddess put her hand under Nima's arm and effortlessly drew her to a standing position. Tingles of energy ran from the spot where Renenutet held Nima upright with inhuman strength. Passing through her body in torrents, the sensation fizzed and sparked, settling in her injured ankle. Pain assaulted Nima as the injured muscles and tendons knit back together. She bit her lip to keep from crying out.

In an attempt to distract herself from the healing process, she blurted out a question. "How—how are you here? The Hyksos boasted to me no Egyptian Great One could enter this place because of their god's spell."

Laughing so hard the black plumes on her crown shook, the goddess released her and stepped back. "These *males*—gods and humans—they always think they rule the world, forgetting I'm an Elemental Elder goddess, born in the start of time. I have powers and abilities the modern ones like Qemtusheb and Horus fail to consider." She raised a finger. "They forget my creatures own the cracks and crevices of the earth. Let foolish men block access above ground or through the sky—I can't be deterred so easily. Luckily for them and all their schemes, I prefer my own duties to their endless quest for power and dominance."

The door crashed open, startling Nima. Sword at the ready, the guard stepped across the threshold. "Who are you talking to—"

Turning her head, Renenutet snapped her fingers, and the man fell dead in a boneless heap, his sword clattering away across the stone floor. Nima ran to the corpse, swallowing her nausea, and wrenched his belt knife from its sheath despite her shaking hands.

"What is it you want of me this time, girl?" the goddess asked, toying with the bracelet of snakes.

"Escape from here." Nima's answer came without conscious thought, as she stared down the torchlit hall. She gripped the carved bone handle of the knife, knuckles white, as she turned back to her patron goddess. "To reunite with Kamin."

Renenutet nodded. "Time grows short for all things in this place. As you wish, take back the remaining snakes of Nebu and use them."

"Forgive me, my lady, but I don't understand. Use them how?"

Renenutet clasped her hand over Nima's, and the snakes slithered one by one onto her wrist, where they reformed themselves into an elegant bracelet. The goddess's fingers were icy cold, her grip strong. "Think what it is you wish each snake to be, to accomplish. Although you have forfeited two already, the final three may achieve your heart's desire. Now listen carefully. There is a side gate to this fortress, where they send men two or three at a time to the river below this plateau, for water, to hunt game and the like. When you reach the main courtyard, turn left, and this single gate will be at the juncture of the walls."

"Unguarded?" Nima asked.

Withdrawing her hand from Nima's, the goddess smoothed down the intricate pleats in her iridescent gown. "You have a knife. You have my snakes. Nuit hung the full moon in her sky tonight, which will guide you to the river at the base of the plateau. Follow the river's course to the Nile." Green light blazed in the cell, surrounding Renenutet, who morphed into a giant black cobra between one heartbeat and the next. Golden hood flared out, she slithered around Nima's body once, ruby-red tongue flickering to kiss Nima's forehead. Then the giant serpent shot straight at the stone wall like an arrow. Renenutet disappeared into an impenetrable black inkiness just before she reached the barrier, the black cloud winking out as soon as her tail passed into the gloom.

Knees weak, Nima adjusted her grip on the knife and slunk into the hallway past the dead guard, afraid if she hesitated for even an instant she'd be found out. Or lose her courage. She made it to the courtyard without trouble, relieved that the goddess had made her ankle as good as new. The halls were empty, the soldiers in their barracks. Apparently, General Nebuchazz had no concerns about any internal threats. When she reached the parade ground, Nima paused in the shadow of a column and reconnoitered. The guards on the wall were patrolling, gazing out across the flanks of the mountain, but lax discipline seemed to be the rule elsewhere as the two men standing at the main gate were leaning on their spears and talking.

I should be able to reach the door the goddess described easily. And I can wish one of these snakes into becoming the golden key. Yet Nima didn't move toward freedom. Fingering the knife, she glanced at the glittering ruby eyes of the snakes around her wrist and pondered. Once out of the fort, even after reaching the river, it was going to be a long, torturous hike to reach the Nile, much less to find her way to the capital city of Tentaris. Would the nomarch believe her wild story? And how would she ever locate Kamin, one soldier among thousands, in Pharaoh's army? She stared at the stacks of shields and spears, the racked bows and full quivers. What Kamin would give to be here now, *inside* the fortress.

Decision made, Nima pushed away from the pillar, straightening her back. *Fire. Fire will cause them the most damage. And I know just the place to set the blaze.* Slinking through the shadows, she headed for the stables, going in the opposite direction of the door to her freedom.

The stable was warm, cozy, redolent of horses and leather. Bales of hay were stacked neatly in the loft above the stalls, just as Nima had hoped. Quickly, she went down the line of horses, untying the knots so the animals would have a chance to run before the fire got too well established. Then she hastened up the rickety ladder to the loft, taking a torch with her. Tossing the firebrand into the farthest corner, she jumped to the stable floor, her restored ankle easily bearing the shock of impact.

Running to the door, she shoved it open before slapping the rump of the nearest horse. Startled, the animal bolted into the courtyard, followed by the horses closest to it. Stepping out of the stampede's path, Nima could hear the fire taking hold above her, hissing and roaring as flames exploded through the dry fodder. Memories of the burning inn at Hebenar rising in her mind, she scurried into the courtyard as men began shouting, and sleepy soldiers poured from the barracks, heading for the stable.

Taking advantage of the chaos, Nima made her way to the main gate, now abandoned by the guards caught up in the panic. Crouching in a shadow, she held the bracelet of snakes in her fingers. "Fire, I command you to become fire and burn this entrance, so the men of Egypt can enter when they arrive." The little reptile hissed in her hand for a moment before disengaging from the other two snakes and slithering to the ground, becoming a rivulet of unearthly green fire as it went.

Satisfied, Nima sprinted along the wall, locating the single door right where Renenutet had said it would be. Breathing hard, she stared into the eyes of the next golden snake. "A key, I command you to become a key for this door!"

The snake wound its sinuous way down her outstretched hand to the keyhole in the single panel door, sliding into the opening and disappearing. Tiny golden sparks jetted out, and there was an audible click. Nima put her hand on the door to push it open just as there were shouts behind her.

"Stop that woman!"

Before she had a chance to open the door more than a few inches, she was grabbed from behind and yanked around to face a furious soldier. "Trying to escape in the chaos, slave?"

"Trying to kill all of you," she said, stabbing him in the chest with the dagger.

Cursing, he dropped his grip on her, but the wound wasn't a killing blow, apparently missing his heart. He staggered forward, grabbing her dress as he fell. Frantically, Nima tugged at the fabric, before kneeling to untangle his fingers or cut herself loose. She wasn't given time as more soldiers ran up to seize her. Kicking, biting and fighting as hard as she could, she was no match for the well-trained warriors, who soon subdued her, one wrapping his belt around her wrists.

"This is no slave—she's the Egyptian prisoner," said the officer in charge when he glimpsed her face in the moonlight .

"The general's dancer? How did she get out here?" asked the man next to him.

"The soldiers in the patrol said she was a witch." Nima's captor spoke up. She could feel a tremor run through his body, but his grip didn't slacken.

"No Hyksos prison can contain me," Nima said. She spat in the officer's face. "You're all going to die when the Egyptian army gets here."

The officer wiped his face with the corner of his cloak. "Bitch! You'll regret this night's work soon enough. Take her to the general."

*****

Impatience and eagerness for battle burning through him, Kamin stared at the fortress, perched on a rise in the small valley below. *I know Nima's in there, I can feel it.* He clenched his fist around the reins. Sensing his mood, the chariot horses took a step or two down the trail until he yanked them to a halt with one swift tug.

"Not yet," he said.

His companion, Tiy-Ineb-Menhet , nomarch of this province, glanced at him. "Soon, my friend. The men are almost in position, and then we go."

Who knows how much time she has left down there? Urgency, underscored by an icy thread of fear, pounded in Kamin's veins. He wasn't afraid for himself. No member of Pharaoh's Own Regiment went into combat with an unsettled mind. He'd long ago made peace with the idea of his own death, put it aside in his heart and mind so he could be at his most effective, undeterred by fear. He knew to the core of his being he could depend on his own skills and those of his comrades. Fate was in the gods' hands. But Nima was another story entirely. She was no highly trained combat veteran. There was no one inside that hellish compound who would stand at her side, protect her.

Nima, I'm so close to you now. Hang on!

He assessed the massed troops he and the nomarch led. Closest to the chariot was the small unit of Pharaoh's own men, sent to fight under Tiy's command, some in chariots, some on foot. *The deadly tip of the spear.* Then the well-trained local troops, whipped into shape by Tiy and his officers from Thebes. They'd easily taken out the enemy sentinels along the trail, men grown lax and careless after so long in the desert with no real danger.

For the thousandth time, Kamin laid a hand on the small leather pouch attached to his belt, reassured at the touch of the special amulet waiting there, his intended gift to Nima. He refused to accept any idea she wasn't alive in that grim keep across the valley.

The nomarch's personal battle flag, the shield symbol overlaid with the cartouche of Horus, snapped and waved in the predawn breeze. A falcon shrieked overhead, but when Kamin tilted his head back to search for the bird, there was no sign of the aerial watcher.

"We'll find her, sir, don't worry," said the grizzled sergeant standing next to the standard-bearer. "Every man in the ranks knows we're looking for an Egyptian woman, a prisoner whose life must be preserved at all costs."

Kamin nodded his thanks. Tiy had been thorough in posting an order listing preservation of Nima's life as the top priority, just behind the defeat of the Hyksos army. Half smiling, he looked at the fortress again, remembering Nima drawing the map for him in the sand not so long ago. *She had it all correct, too, right down to the hills surrounding this place.*

"What in the name of the gods is happening?" Kamin grabbed the nomarch's arm and pointed as a huge plume of yellow and orange flames billowed over the fortress. Strange green fire lit up the gates.

"Could be your lady is causing chaos," Tiy said.

An officer approached the chariot, saluting Tiy and Kamin. "We're ready, sirs, battering ram in place."

"We go then." Tiy raised his arm, sword pointed defiantly at the sky, and brought it down to point at the enemy target ahead. "Charge!"

Trumpets blared. Cracking his long whip, Kamin gave his horses their heads and the chariot lurched into rapid movement down the mountain road, heading for the gates. Beside him, the Regiment's best archer launched arrow after arrow toward the sentries walking the ramparts, taking out a man with each shot. More chariots swept down the road behind Kamin's. The cart carrying the heavy battering ram rumbled along in their wake, soldiers trotting beside it, shields at the ready.

The burning gates fell outward off their hinges, and a small wave of enemy warriors boiled onto the small plain, clashing with the Egyptian troops in individual battles.

Funnel of death, Kamin thought in grim satisfaction. *Rush out here one by one, you fools, and let us pick you off.*

Unchallenged, Kamin drove the chariot through the entrance into the first ring of defenses. He and Tiy jumped down from the vehicle, swords and shields at the ready, and joined the battle. Confused Hyksos warriors who had been firefighting were slow to reach their weapons. The courtyard was tightly packed with chariots and other gear, which also impeded the defenders' efforts. Loose horses galloped here and there, further compounding the chaos.

The archer stayed close to Kamin, as ordered, bow slung as he wielded his sword with deadly effect. Other men from the special unit fought to keep the Hyksos from overwhelming Kamin or the nomarch.

Screaming curses and orders, a Hyksos officer rallied his troops, sending men to weak points in the defenses. The voice of command drew Kamin's attention.

Kamin thought he recognized Amarkash. "Son of a jackal!" Sword raised, jumping over bodies, dodging pairs of grim combatants, Kamin ran across the courtyard, intercepted by another enemy officer in a violent clash of swords and shields. The man fought well, thrust and parry and attack, but Kamin was desperate to get past him, to find out if it had indeed been Amarkash he'd glimpsed. *I can force him to reveal where Nima is, then wring the bastard's neck.*

Going on the offensive, his opponent raised his round leather shield, strangely shaped sword slashing at Kamin's shield, denting the surface with the power of his blows.

Focus now, or this man in front of you will kill you and you'll fail Nima. Maintaining concentration in battle wasn't normally a problem for Kamin, but today crippling fear gripped him. What if she already lay dead or dying?

Clearing his mind of doubt, he shoved the warrior away with a powerful punch just below the chin, using his own shield. Stepping forward, he launched a flurry of hacking blows, driving the officer first to his knees then to the ground, then slashing his neck right above the leather breastplate, the energy of combat and fear for Nima giving Kamin superhuman strength.

When he looked up, jerking his bloody sword free of the corpse, Kamin saw that Tiy had the battering-ram unit hard at work on the doors to the inner areas of the fortress. Arrows and debris rained down from the walls above, but the shield-bearers protected the men working the battering ram. Out of the corner of his eye, Kamin saw Amarkash break away.

"To me!" Kamin yelled at the Egyptian soldiers nearest him, gesturing with his bloody sword as he vaulted over dying men and ran into the fortress through the door Amarkash had used. Yet another courtyard awaited him, a third ring in the defenses, empty of foot soldiers, although arrows flew from the few archers left on the battlements. A huge portal barred the way to the main portion of the fortress. Breathing hard, blood trickling down his arm from a glancing sword wound, Kamin paused, assessing the situation.

"Stand back, sir." The archer drew him aside as the battering ram rolled forward through the hole its crew had created in the previous wall. The huge log burned in a few spots, and soldiers beat at the flames with their cloaks.

Tiy came to him, uniform bloodstained, his personal guards close beside him. "You took off like a gazelle."

"Thought I saw the man who held Nima and me prisoner. He ducked through this last gate." Tying a rag around the wound in his arm while they waited for the men to breach the door, Kamin fastened the knot with his teeth.

*****

Nebuchazz was waiting, clad only in a loose blue-striped robe and a loincloth, his face contorted in anger as he stared out the window at the burning stables and smoldering gates. Swinging around as the man entered the room, dragging Nima, the general walked to his desk and sat. "So, you do have power, as the priest claimed," he said. "And your ankle has healed, apparently."

"I'm not dancing for you or your misbegotten god," Nima said, struggling to jerk free of the man who held her arms. She tossed her head to shift her disheveled hair off her face. She could hear distant sounds of battle, which gave her hope.

Nebuchazz rose, came around the desk and smoothed her hair away from her cheeks. He leaned close, eyes staring directly into her eyes, his breath puffing in her face as he spoke. "No, you're not going to dance for him," he said in a reasonable tone of voice. "You're going to die on his altar later today for your crimes. But the god won't begrudge me a few hours of pleasure first." He nuzzled her cheek, the stubble on his cheeks rasping on her smooth skin, while she squirmed in the soldier's grasp. "I'll have time to enact all my fantasies about you, little dancer." Cupping her chin for a moment, he planted a wet kiss on her lips before stepping away. "Take her to my bedchamber and tie her to the bed to await my attention after we get the fires out."

Nima twisted her wrists against the belt restraining her, getting a grip on the last snake. "Poison to his heart," she screamed.

The snake vanished from her wrist. The general paused in midstep, turned slowly to stare at her, his face going blank, his lips opening in an exclamation of surprise even as they blackened from the poison. He clutched at his chest, crumpling to the floor in a heap, purple foam spewing from his mouth. With an audible cracking of bones, he convulsed once before he lay still.

The soldier holding her practically threw Nima across the room, so anxious was he to be safely away from her. "Witch, you're a witch," he yelled, drawing his sword. He started forward as Nima searched frantically for another way out of the room, or anything she could grab for self-defense.

"Hold!" Amarkash rushed into the room, blocking the soldier's sword with a rapid thrust of his own, disarming the man. "What in the name of the seven hells has gone on here?"

The soldier tried to tell him, his curses and explanations loud and panicky.

Amarkash spun around to stare at Nima. "So you *are* a being of power, just as the priest insisted you had to be." Rubbing his cheek, where an angry red slash throbbed, he winced. For the first time, Nima noticed a bloody bandage covering his upper arm. "Your Egyptians have broken into the first ring of defenses, assisted by the chaos you've created. Your cursed army and the general leading them fight as if possessed by powers greater than mortal men." He pushed Nebuchazz's contorted corpse with a cautious toe, then grinned. "Seems I'm in command now. I can snatch glorious victory from defeat by sacrificing you and invoking all the power of Qemtusheb," Amarkash said, striding to the door. "Bring her."

Two priests who had entered the room on his heels hustled her out, the soldier trailing behind. Nima twisted and kicked, but they easily kept her under control, forcing her to walk. "Killing me isn't going to do you any good."

Amarkash paused for a minute, glancing over his shoulder at her. "Our plans have gone wrong since the first moment Nebuchazz watched you dance and became obsessed with owning you. I wonder if your gods used you to thwart our intentions. I think your death on the altar will go a long way to making up for all the trouble you've caused." He issued crisp orders to the young priests. "Carry her if you must. We're running out of time. The ceremony can only be foreshortened so much if it's to work."

The man on the left snatched her up in his arms, running after Amarkash as he broke into a sprint down the hall. Huffing and puffing, adjusting his elaborately embroidered ceremonial robes as he went, another, much older priest joined them. Nima continued her attempts to make the priest drop her, but he adjusted his hold, slinging her over one shoulder like a sheaf of wheat and kept striding. Leaving the corridors she'd seen before, they briefly crossed the far side of the courtyard, where Egyptian soldiers now did battle with Hyksos warriors at the top of the wall. Instinctively, she screamed for Kamin.

He must be there in the front ranks, trying to get to me.

CHAPTER ELEVEN

BOOM!

Louder than thunder, the sound of the battering ram's impact on the stout wooden panels echoed in the courtyard. Swinging in its chains as the crew rolled it forward again and again, the giant tree trunk assaulted the final defense. Kamin watched, breathing hard, regaining his strength for the next surge of combat once the gate was breached. With a tremendous splintering sound, the portal collapsed, remnants dangling from the bronze hinges. Men scurried to drag the battering ram out of the way. Kamin plunged through the opening first, nimbly picking a path through the debris, followed by the archer, then the nomarch and the rest of the troops.

Kamin hesitated. Amarkash was his intended quarry. His only target. Suddenly, he heard someone scream his name. Wheeling in the direction of the sound, he saw the Hyksos warriors retreating into the main building. Sprinting in that direction, Kamin skidded to a stop as the massive door slammed in his face.

"Bring the battering ram!" he yelled, gesturing with his sword.

Tiy joined him, eyeing the door and the courtyard critically. "Not sure we can get the necessary momentum in this space."

Kamin banged his fist on the wood in sheer frustration. *So close.* "Nima's in there. I heard her scream. "

"No time to waste then." Tiy gestured to his men, and they began repositioning the massive ram to make a run at this new obstacle, while the other soldiers established a perimeter.

One collision with the ram was enough to crash through the last door, which had clearly not been constructed to keep out hostile troops. Again, Kamin was first through the opening, the archer at his side.

*****

The priest carrying her ducked through a side door, narrowly avoiding a flight of black Egyptian arrows coming their way.

The older priest had gone ahead. Amarkash and the solder lowered a thick slab of wood to bar the door behind them before sprinting alongside Nima's captor, through the new corridor. They came out on an open terrace cut into the side of the mountain. It was huge, with room enough for easily one hundred people to stand.

The priest paused, allowing Nima to slide down his body and stand on her own two feet.

Heart pounding, she examined her surroundings, hoping for something she could use as a weapon, some means of defense or escape. A round stone dominated the terrace. Nima had never seen anything like it—easily eight feet long, with elaborate carvings along the base. Glittering in the dawn sunlight as if tiny diamonds lay buried below the surface, there was something hypnotizing about the altar. She screwed her eyes shut for a moment, shaking her head. The guard jerked her forward by the wrists. The old priest took up a position between the stone and the terrace railing, next to a claw-footed table holding candles, statues, and incense. Already chanting to their god Qemtusheb, he faced the rising sun.

"Bring her to the altar," Amarkash said in a low voice, gesturing impatiently.

I've got to delay them, stall as long as I can. Twisting and struggling, Nima tried to dig in, to pull away, but the young priest was more than a match for her.

Knife in hand, Amarkash waited. "What a pity we won't be able to continue our sessions with my ropes, dancer. Watching you die will be pleasurable in its own way, however."

"You're sick. All of you are as evil as the filthy god you worship." Nima spat in his face.

He wiped his cheek with his sleeve, unperturbed, and stepped forward. As the priests held her between them, Amarkash slit her dress from neck to hem and tore it from her body. Nima stood nearly naked before him, clad only in her undergarments, shivering in the morning breezes.

"There's no time to perform the ritual purification or garb you in sacrificial robes," Amarkash said.

"Killing me buys you nothing. You and your god will lose this war." Nima stood tall, heedless of her near nudity.

Amarkash stepped aside, pointing to the altar. "Lay her in place on the stone and help me fasten the restraints."

Fighting them every inch of the way, she was placed on the smooth surface of the sacrificial stone. Trying to scramble off the altar, Nima was mesmerized by ripples of molten red light streaking through the stone. The surface was oddly warm, sticky, with something pulsing below her as if a living heart beat inside the block. Her skin crawled and itched wherever her body touched the stone, which felt like the pelt of a living creature. *What demon is locked inside this altar?* The priests and Amarkash forced her onto her back, spread eagle, snapping heavy shackles over her wrists and ankles, pinning her tightly to the rock.

The old priest slowly turned and continued his chanting, stepping close to the altar at Nima's head.

Tugging futilely at the restraints, Nima realized there was no escape now. She closed her eyes. *Kamin.* The burning pain of a hard slap across the face had her jerking against the chains, her eyes opening against her will. Amarkash was nose to nose with her, his flushed face radiating hatred. "I want you to see the embrace of Qemtusheb as the god takes you, uses you to defeat your own people. He'll destroy your lover if he's out there."

Summoning all her courage, praying to whichever Great One might listen, Nima remembered Kamin's eyes, so defiant, so undefeated, at the beginning of this journey, the first time she'd met him. "Do your worst, then. I know you and your god will fail." She felt calm, weightless, as if nothing happening in the chamber of death could touch her, as if she stood to the side watching. Relaxing in the restraints, she took a deep breath as the high priest raised his knife over her, chanting the words of his petition to Qemtusheb in hypnotic repetition.

The scream of an enraged falcon echoed through the room. Startled, Nima craned her neck as much as she could, to see a massive bird of prey diving toward the terrace, lethal talons extended to rend and tear. Rainbow sparks glinted from the diamond pupils of its uncanny eyes. Cringing, the high priest broke off his song and ducked away from the altar, placing his back to the nearest solid wall and covering his face with one arm.

Amarkash stood fast, gesturing to the slack-jawed soldier. "Shoot the damn thing. What are you waiting for?"

The falcon broke off its attack as if it had encountered some obstacle. Shrieking defiance, the bird soared aloft and came diving through the air again. The Hyksos archer shot a volley of arrows, all of which fell short as if deflected by a shield. Nima held her breath as the bird tried to cross the edge of the terrace and savage the enemy, but once more, it back winged and shot away, prevented from reaching her.

"The power of Qemtusheb holds firm," the oldest priest said with relief, wiping his brow. "The bird is unable to penetrate this consecrated space." Stepping to the altar, he noisily cleared his throat, sacrificial knife clenched in his palsied hand. "Where was I? Do we have any of the sacred herb wine to calm my nerves?"

"There's no time for you to get drunk," Amarkash said, glancing from the altar where Nima was pinned, to the door across the room, which vibrated and groaned under the Egyptian assault from the other side. "Kill the girl now and summon the god to help us."

A massive crash and shouting at the other end of the room drew everyone's attention. Faltering, the elderly priest lowered the knife for a moment. Cursing, Amarkash strode out of Nima's range of vision. She heard shouting in both languages, but she kept her eyes on the priest.

"Please," she said. "You've lost. Don't do this."

*****

Following the angry cries of a falcon, troops at his heels, Kamin burst into a room the likes of which he'd never seen before. Screams of rage from the bird drew Kamin's attention to the far side, where a waist-high, circular black altar loomed and Amarkash stood with priests and soldiers. Nima lay chained to the altar as a priest raised his gleaming sacrificial knife. Without conscious thought, Kamin dropped his sword, yanked the bow from the man standing next to him, and shot the priest through the heart.

"Amarkash, you son of a bitch, face me now," he yelled. Grabbing his sword, Kamin ran forward, barely conscious of the others at his heels. The Hyksos captain drew his weapon, and Kamin saw the flicker of recognition when Amarkash recognized his recent captive.

"Ah, the lover," he sneered. "You abandoned your woman in the middle of the desert and now you come to reclaim her? I'll slaughter you first, and then her blood will stain the altar, bringing Qemtusheb to give us victory."

"You got one thing right. You have to kill me first," Kamin taunted, anxious to keep the enemy's attention on him. "If you're skillful enough."

Amarkash adjusted his leather shield and bounded forward, his sword meeting Kamin's in a violent clash of metal. Kamin whirled and got in a blow before his off-balance opponent could recover. The Hyksos's leather tunic protected him to some extent, but blood spurted where Kamin's sword had landed. Without mercy, Kamin pressed his advantage.

Tiring, Amarkash retreated toward the altar, stumbling over another corpse.

Afraid of what the man might do to Nima, Kamin outflanked his opponent, forcing him away from the stone. Apparently calling on some inner reserve, Amarkash tried to go on the offensive, but his strength waned. Kamin sidestepped the assault, bringing his sword around with enough force to sever Amarkash's head.

Breathing hard, Kamin staggered to the altar and hurled the gruesome corpse of the priest he'd shot away from Nima, letting the man's body slide to the floor. Unfastening his scarlet cloak, he prepared to swathe his beloved in its folds to shield her bruised, battered body from anyone else's eyes. *Horus, please, let us have been in time.*

*****

The world spun around Nima, confused glimpses of battle, sounds of anger and fear. In his dying throes the priest had plunged his knife into her shoulder and then fallen across her upper body, where he lay for long moments, his grotesque face turned toward her, sightless eyes wide, his blood mingling with hers on her bare shoulder. She knew men fought viciously beside the altar. Kamin, dueling with Amarkash, moved in and out of her limited range of vision, sword slashing in a battle to the death. She thought other Egyptian soldiers thronged the chamber, skirmishing with the priests and Hyksos, judging by the noise and the cursing in both languages.

Am I hallucinating from the incense and loss of blood? Dizzy, she shut her eyes against the view of the dead priest, until suddenly his body was yanked off her, Egyptian curses filling the air.

"Hang on, beloved, stay with me." Bending over the altar, Kamin draped his cloak across her nearly naked, bloodied body. "You've been so brave, so strong. You can't die."

The restraints were struck from her wrists and ankles. In the next moment, Kamin lifted her in his strong arms, wrapped in the cloak, and held her close against his pounding heart. "Bring a doctor!"

She tried to raise her hand to caress his face but had no strength left. "Kamin," she whispered.

Eyes narrowed, jaw set, he brushed a kiss on her lips. "Don't talk. Save your energy." Raising his head, he spoke to whoever surrounded them, frustration and anger in his voice. "Where in the seven hells is that damn doctor? I ordered him to stay close." Kamin cradled her tenderly. "We have to stop the bleeding."

"I—I tried to be brave, for you." She touched his chin with the tips of her trembling fingers. She believed he kissed her hand, but the world went black, vision and hearing fading away.

"Nima, wake up. Don't leave me." Kamin swallowed against the lump in his throat, studying her pale, bruised face. He could see the pulse beating in the hollow of her neck, which was somewhat reassuring. Keeping pressure on her wound to stem the bleeding, he raised his voice again. "The doctor is a dead man if he doesn't arrive in the next breath. Where is the fool?"

"Here, my lord, let me examine the patient." The Egyptian physician pushed his way through the group of men and bent to examine the jagged slash in Nima's shoulder.

Tiy laid a hand on Kamin's shoulder. "Perhaps if you bring her over to the long table by the side wall, the doctor can perform his treatment more effectively. I know you don't want to be parted from her, but we have to finish mopping up the resistance in the fortress. She'll be safe here under physician Djal's care, and I need you elsewhere."

After the nomarch swept the surface clean of candles and containers, Kamin did as suggested, tenderly placing Nima on the low table against the side wall. The doctor immediately cleansed the ugly wound, after which he spread a sweet-smelling herbal paste on it. Kamin paced along the line of soldiers, staring into each man's eyes for a moment before moving on to the next warrior. "This woman is my life. Her bravery is the only reason we found this fortress. Swear to me you'll guard her as fiercely as I would—"

The burly sergeant, his Pharaoh's Own Regiment badge gleaming, saluted and spoke for all of them. "No harm will come to her while any of us draw breath, sir."

Nodding in agreement, the other men in the squad formed a half circle around Nima and the doctor, facing outward into the room, swords drawn and ready, shields raised to form a barricade against attack.

"I want her out of this hellhole as soon as she can be safely moved," Kamin said, looking to see what progress the doctor was making.

"I'll personally oversee the lady's transfer to a tent in our encampment," the sergeant answered. Stepping closer to Kamin, the grizzled soldier lowered his voice. "She's one of us now, sir, given what she did for Egypt, and you know we protect our own."

Putting his hand on the other man's shoulder for a moment, Kamin nodded his thanks. "You give my mind some ease."

"Come, my friend." Tiy gestured with his sword. "Work remains to be done here."

Kamin ran his hands through his hair, glancing hungrily at Nima one more time before wheeling to glare at the altar. "Aye, and this cursed black stone is one question. We can't allow the altar to remain as a magnet for evil or a shrine for any other adherents of Qemtusheb, once our army has withdrawn."

Tiy walked toward the blood-soaked stone, Kamin a few paces behind. "I could leave a detachment stationed out here to watch over it, but I don't much like the idea. I don't have men to spare right now, and the site is so isolated."

A falcon swooped in to sit on the terrace railing, Kamin and the nomarch swinging around to face it. Gliding from the rail, the bird morphed into a man in midair, standing tall and fierce as his golden sandals hit the floor. Arriving without sword or shield this time, the god still wore the towering red and white crown and a warrior's uniform and breastplate. Horus's eyes remained the moon and sun, casting light and color in his godly guise.

Kamin went to one knee, his friend the nomarch following suit. "Lord Horus."

"So, warrior," the god said to Kamin, smiling a little. "Did I keep our bargain to your satisfaction? The woman lives. I battered my wings against the barriers of evil at the end to distract them while you broke down the door."

"I am ever grateful, my lord," Kamin answered. "I only pray she survives the priest's dying blow."

Horus stared beyond them, seeking out the spot where Nima lay unconscious. "Your woman has the heart of a warrior. I've taken her under my wing; she'll survive today's events. " He raised one hand. "Hear my decree and promise—I'll attend the judgment of your heart and hers in the Afterlife and speak as your witness when that day comes. Your hearts beat as one now and neither shall be left to mourn the other when your allotted days in the Black Lands are complete."

Kamin struggled to find the words to express his gratitude for this unprecedented honor. "You bestow a rare blessing, Great One."

But the god apparently had a new concern. Frowning, Horus contemplated the altar. "Once your army has departed, I'll deal with the destruction of this bloodstained stone. I'll call upon Anubis and the goddess Nephthys, and together we'll blast this abomination into the lake of fire, close the door Qemtusheb's priests partially opened. Let no man or woman remain behind, or they too will die."

The nomarch nodded. "As you command, Great One. Thank you for ridding my province of this evil talisman."

Horus made a dismissive gesture. "Go now, finish the human business of conquering this fortress. Depart at first light tomorrow morning. I'll stand guard over the altar stone tonight to ensure no minions of evil penetrate the Red or Black Lands before we can lay waste to the entire area."

Kamin and Tiy bowed to acknowledge the god's command. In a heartbeat, Horus disappeared from the terrace, becoming a massive falcon who flew to drift in lazy circles on the thermal currents rising from the valley floor outside the fortress.

"Are we the only ones aware of the Great One, then?" Kamin asked, glancing at the squad of soldiers to the side of the room.

"Horus must have willed it so. Interesting company you kept in the desert, my friend," Tiy said to Kamin as they hastened from the altar room to supervise the final surrender of the garrison. "Perhaps one man in a million receives a promise from the gods to stand witness to his worthiness for entrance to the Afterlife, unless he be a Pharoah." Tiy shot a quick sideways glance at him. "You know, you're the last man in our company of comrades I'd have picked to marry a dancer. Your Nima must be rare indeed. I'm eager to become better acquainted with her."

"Just don't ask her to dance for you." Kamin drew his sword as they quickened their pace to join an ongoing skirmish at the far wall. "I've learned I'm an extremely jealous man."

*****

Nima awoke on a clean bed, covered by a soft linen sheet in a small tent by herself. Her shoulder was bandaged but throbbed and hurt, which stopped her from shifting too much under the sheet. She wore a plain beige linen nightgown, and a fringed blue and green shawl lay across her chest.

"Ah, excellent, you're finally awake." A strange man stood in the entrance to the tent, black lacqured box of instruments and nostrums dangling by an ivory handle from one hand. *A doctor, thank the gods. Perhaps he can give me something to blunt the pain in my shoulder.* With deep relief, she glimpsed Egyptian soldiers standing guard beyond him before the tent flap fell shut.

Lying against a smooth wooden headrest, she considered his words, puzzling over which question to ask first. "What did you mean *finally?* How long have I been unconscious?"

"Three days." He came to the bed to take her pulse with cool hands, check her forehead for fever. "I am Djal, physician to the nomarch."

"Where are we?" She was relieved to see that, although the tent was sparsely furnished, it was unmistakably Egyptian. "Not—not at the Hyksos fortress?"

He shook his head. "No indeed, you are with the nomarch's army, traveling to his capital city of Tentaris after the great victory. The men carry you in a shaded litter during the day's march, surrounded by a special force of guards. From Pharaoh's Own Regiment, mind you." The doctor clucked his tongue in awe at the honor she'd been accorded. "I attend you closely at all times, as ordered. And General Kaminhotep comes throughout the day to check on you. He sits with you through the night, until it is time for camp to be struck in the morning and the march to resume. He'll be relieved to find you so improved tonight."

"General?" *What do I have to do with an Egyptian general?* Pulse quickening, a small trickle of fear ran along her nerves.

The doctor nodded, his eyes narrowed. "You were unaware of his rank? They tell me he travels undercover sometimes as part of his duties for Pharaoh. Perhaps he felt it unwise to reveal his true identity to you when you were both prisoners?" He stepped away to a long table at the other side of the tent, opening jars and small baskets, pulling out ingredients according to a recipe on a small papyrus scroll he took from his belt pouch.

Busy mixing a potion for her to drink, the chatty doctor added an aside over his shoulder. "The general is Pharaoh's cousin as well, served with Nat-re-Akhte since before he ascended to the throne. Pharaoh holds him in high regard and trust. An excellent connection for me to make, thanks to you. He'll be grateful for my skills."

The doctor rambled on about his hopes for an appointment to the royal court based on his care for Nima. She stopped paying attention to his social-climbing plans. She lay still to avoid disturbing her shoulder and bringing on the waves of pain. Focusing on the seams in the roof of the tent, she tried to make sense of this new information.

Kamin, high-ranking? A noble related to royalty? Tears pricked in Nima's eyes. Not a humble soldier suitable in station for a tavern dancer to marry. *Why didn't he tell me?* Why did he let me dream? Angrily, she brushed the moisture from her cheek with her good hand. She didn't know whether to be angry, terrified or distraught at the prospect of what he might offer to one such as her. Her thoughts whirled until her head ached and she grew dizzy with anxiety. *I love him with all my heart, but I vowed never to take a concubine's position in any man's house. Do I have the strength to refuse him?*

Numbly, she drank the nasty concoction Djal handed her. *Don't doctors have any potions with a pleasing taste? Would honeyed medicine violate some secret oath?* Impatiently, not waiting for his potion to take effect, he unwrapped the bandages on her shoulder to examine and cleanse her wound, and the hurried motion added nausea to the dizziness already assailing her. Her breathing became labored, the fears about her future causing her chest to grow tight. A sharp stab of pain all through her upper body as the physician probed the wound was the final insult, making the world reel, and Nima passed out.

*****

When she came to again, cool twilight had fallen, and a soft breeze whispered through the open door of the tent. Oil lamps provided gentle illumination. The remnants of a barely touched meal sat ignored on a table close to the bed. Kamin perched on a stool by her bedside, holding her hand in a loose but comforting grip. He wore a heavy gold signet ring, a falcon set with diamond eyes flying under a complicated cartouche. Deep in thought, he studied a papyrus in his other hand.

He's tired. Nima watched him for a minute, heart aching with love tempered by the loss of her dreams of a simple life together. Confirming the doctor's tale, Kamin was in a general's uniform, crisp, white, pleated kilt edged in gold, cinched with a broad leather belt inlaid with more gold, jewels set in the buckle. He wore a leopard skin over the kilt. Leather straps crossed his broad, muscular chest, and the golden falcon badge of Pharaoh's Own Regiment gleamed in the center. His black and gold *nemes* headcloth had been laid aside, on the foot of her cot, along with the golden flail of an officer. She hardly recognized this imposing person as the man she had journeyed with, danced for, and made love to.

His head came up as she shifted on the hard mattress. He inhaled sharply, eyes sparkling, the little crinkles appearing around them as he grinned and tossed the scroll on the foot of the bed so he could take both of her hands in his. "At last you're awake. I feared the obsequious doctor was lying to me."

Her heart skipped a beat at the tender concern on his face, and for a moment she couldn't speak for the lump in her throat. She licked her dry lips. "Thank you for rescuing me, my lord."

Pressing a kiss into her palm, he searched her face. "What is this sudden formality? I'm still Kamin to you—"

"But not exactly an ordinary soldier." She gestured at the *nemes* and the golden flail. "You command armies, don't you?"

"Well, yes, sometimes, but I don't see what my rank has to do with the love between us." He reached out to wipe away a tear on her cheek with his callused thumb. "Are you in pain? I can get the doctor—"

She shook her head, swiping at her eyes. "No, the pain is bearable, and the doctor—"

"Is unbearable. I know," Kamin joked. "But he was trained in Thebes and is the best we have. Only the highest-quality care for you, beloved."

Swallowing hard, Nima tried again to explain her reservations to him. "My lord, I—I dance in *taverns*—"

"And trained as a thief and an assassin." He kissed her hand, but his eyes never left her face, lines of worry on his. "Boredom won't be an issue, I know for a certainty." He rubbed his flat stomach with the other hand. "And I'll eat well, once you instruct my estate's cooks in your knowledge. We'll have to discuss limits on the use of the more exotic herbs, however."

She refused to be sidetracked by his gentle teasing. "You're Pharaoh's cousin. You can't marry someone like me. I'd bring ridicule and disgrace to your house. You have to marry a grand lady of the court."

"The foolish doctor talks entirely too much." Frowning, Kamin rubbed the back of his neck. "He's treading on thin ground with me, skilled physician or not. I can marry whoever I choose, and it pleases me to marry you." He kissed her forehead. "I love you, as you might recall. I went through hell when I realized you'd left me at the oasis to draw Amarkash off. Had Horus himself not stood in my way, I'd have come after you then. I bargained with the god, so I could have time to bring the army to your rescue."

"You bargained with a Great One on my behalf?" Dizziness swamped her at the mere idea. Encountering Horus in falcon form had been frightening enough for her. *And Kamin took such a risk for me!* "How did you dare?"

Tenderly, her lover pushed the tangled hair from her face, stroked her cheek with the back of his hand. "I once told you if I was fighting for you, I could do anything."

She coughed a little, her throat scratchy and dry. "But to argue with Horus—"

"Well, I couldn't argue one woman's life was more important than the fate of Egypt. Admitting the fact to the god tore a hole in my heart." Kamin rose to pour her a mug of water, coming to sit on his stool again, raising her to drink, supporting her with one rock-solid arm behind her back.

She sipped gratefully, conscious of his immense strength and how careful he was with her. "The safety of the Black Lands matters more than either you or I. So, on what point did you negotiate?"

Accepting the mug since she was done with the water, he set it on the wicker table. "I asked him to intervene, to delay Amarkash on the road."

"Oh," she said, understanding now. "We had endless problems on the trip. Horses died, wheels fell off the chariots, we were overrun by not one but two sandstorms. The soldiers grumbled I was a witch. The priest of Qemtusheb was convinced I had some power, and then the problems the battalion experienced made everyone a believer."

"I don't think the gods are subtle when they play games with human affairs." He paused, taking a deep breath. "When we stormed their fortress and I saw you stretched on the altar, the damned priest with his knife poised—"Unable to speak, he passed a hand over his face. Nima glimpsed the depth of his raw emotion, betrayed by the gleam of moisture in his eyes. Kamin straightened, rolling his shoulders, jaw clenched. "I would have sought death myself, in battle, if you had died. I would have slaughtered every Hyksos in the fortress, starting with Amarkash, until one of them slew me." He flashed the brash grin Nima loved so much. "Well, I did kill him, by the way, and took pleasure in doing so. But had you died, you'd have been properly avenged, I promise."

Pride made her heart beat faster. "So romantic." She fluttered her eyelashes at him.

He grunted. "Well, I don't know about that, but I'll not live without you." He placed her hand over his heart, his eyes staring directly into hers. "My heart beats for you."

"Definitely romantic," she murmured, drawing him closer for a long kiss.

When the embrace ended, he squared his shoulders, meeting her eyes resolutely. "I'm sorry I didn't tell you more about myself while we were on the run. I understand you might be angry with me."

"It's all right. I'm sure you had good reasons." Smiling, Nima squeezed his hand. "You apologized to me at the caravan, remember? I understood the situation. Not about your glorious title perhaps, but the need for discretion."

"We had more important concerns at the time than my lineage." He raised an eyebrow, and she nodded. "You did point out yourself the less you knew of me and my mission the better, should you be recaptured. I'd determined to claim you as my bride anyway, once I'd gotten you to safety and could do some proper wooing. Get you used to my titles."

"Titles? More than one?" she asked in dismay, the dizziness threatening to return. "The doctor said you were related to Pharaoh."

He shrugged. "I was afraid if I came out with the information too soon you'd raise barriers between us." Pointing a finger at her accusingly, he grinned. "As you tried to do a few minutes ago, with your needless qualms about your background. Your none-too-charitable opinion of the nobility came through loud and clear when we first conversed after our escape."

"You—you're not anything like the nobles I've met before."

"I should hope not." He leaned forward, framed her face tenderly, his rough soldier's hands gentle on her skin, his hazel eyes narrowed, serious. "Let us be clear now—I want you to be my wife, lady of my estates, mistress of my house, mother of my children. I don't care about anything in your past, not one thing. We start *our* story from the moment you risked bringing water to a fellow prisoner."

She sucked in a breath to protest.

Holding up one hand for silence, he tilted his head. "I respect your past. I'd never deny any of your experiences. Everything you've gone through made you the incredible woman you are, the woman I love, but I'll allow nothing to come between *us*."

I can see how he commands armies. Who could stand against such force of will and personality? Her heart beat faster at the vehemence of his declaration. "All well and good here in the desert, but our stations in life are too far apart for you to—"

Shaking his head, Kamin cut her off, but he was grinning ear to ear now. "Somehow I expected this to come up as your next objection. My old friend and battle comrade Nomarch Tiy-Ineb-Menhet commands this army. Together, we sent a recommendation to Pharaoh asking him to award gold of valor to you for your role in the successful rout of the invasion in Shield province."

"Gold of valor? For me?" Nima could hardly voice the questions. *Only the bravest, the best in the military, receive such awards.*

"I thought you'd be pleased. You earned it. You'll be the only woman at Court, or anywhere in Egypt, with such honors to her name. Pharaoh may decide you're too good for the likes of *me*, sweetheart." From his broad smile, clearly he didn't believe his own warning. "Gold of valor places you above any woman in the Black Lands, save for the queen and one or two high priestesses. If you decided you didn't love me, still you'd have wealth and status and never have to dance for anyone ever again. I don't want you to feel coerced into accepting my proposal of marriage. You—you have choices."

As if I could ever contemplate being with another man but Kamin. She sat speechless for a heartbeat before tugging him to where she could kiss him on the lips without jarring her shoulder too much. Keeping her grip on his arm, she said, "You know I love you, and I'm honored to be your wife, if you're sure."

He nodded, his face growing serious again. "Will you mind living in Thebes? My primary estate lies there. I'm done with undercover missions all over Egypt. This was my last foray, and Pharaoh knows of my decision."

"Giving adventure and intrigue up for me? What about your dread for living a safe life?" she teased a tiny bit, secure in his affections. *If Pharaoh himself approves of me, all the naysayers will be silenced. No one can criticize Kamin for marrying me. I bring the honors to his family name as my dowry.* Joy welled up inside her, making her pulse race. *Me, Nima no-name, of nowhere, with a golden dowry!*

"No regrets," Kamin said. "I'm facing forward, to life with you, a home, children, if the gods are kind. I'll have a role to play at court, supporting Nat-re-Akhte as he rebuilds Egypt. He needs men he can trust at his side." His tone turning contemplative, Kamin shrugged. "Different adventures than any I've ever sought before, but honorable, fulfilling nonetheless."

"Everything I've ever wanted." A warm feeling spread through her, a little rush of pleasure , laced with excitement.

"Yes, I think my plans for us cover the list you recited to me, the first night we sheltered in the sandstone cave." He raised his eyebrows a little, tilting his head and smiling.

Does he remember all my foolish dreaming? Nima felt her cheeks grow warm, knew she was blushing again. "The only thing I truly care about is that we're together."

"Always. " He leaned closer, the mischievous glint in his eyes. "Of course, Pharaoh might ask me to do a small favor for him, a quick trip now and then." He kissed her, his tongue tracing her lips until she parted them. Catching him by the neck with her good arm, she drew him closer. Caressing her breast through the nightgown, Kamin adjusted his position to mold her upper body to his. His hands touched the bandages on her shoulder, and he gentled his touch, pulling back with an effort and a frustrated groan. "Yet again we don't have the right time and place. Thank the gods for the caravan where we had *one* moment of peace. Without their sanctuary for a single night of lovemaking, my frustration would know no bounds."

"I'll dance for you," Nima promised agreeably. "As soon as I'm able."

He hugged her, clearly mindful of not aggravating her wound. "And you'll dance for no other, ever again."

"Only you, I swear." She held up a hand, palm against his chest. "On one condition."

"Name the thing," he commanded, trying and failing to keep a monumental frown on his face, belied by the twinkle in his hazel eyes.

"I must be properly rewarded for my skills," she said demurely, fluttering her lashes. "My audience must demonstrate their appreciation. A dancer requires adulation."

"Have no doubt, now or ever. I'd demonstrate my—appreciation—this moment if you weren't injured." He took her hand and pressed it against his cock, hard and hot under the kilt and loincloth. "The mere memory of your dance has an effect on me."

She rubbed her hand along the impressive length of his shaft. "I heal quickly."

"But we can't lie together tonight," Kamin said, removing her hand and kissing it. "The doctor was most emphatic, and I tend to accept his opinion on this point." He studied her face in the lamplight. "You're pale, bruised. "

She subsided, pouting a little and then smiling to show she wasn't seriously upset. "How many days' march is it to Tentaris?"

"Six or seven, depending whether the gods favor us. An army moves more slowly under the best conditions than you and I did." Kamin gestured at the furnishings in the tent. "Too much gear, too many amenities."

"We certainly had no amenities," she agreed, making a one-handed attempt to adjust the shawl. "I think we walked in circles at times, despite the efforts of the falcons to direct us to the Nile."

"Is the evening air giving you a chill?" Kamin adjusted the shawl more closely for her. "Speaking of the falcons, the Great One Horus said he would stand as your patron from now on."

To go from no patron among the Great Ones to being a favorite of Horus! Amazing. Eyes narrowed, she asked, "He conferred such an honor on me, a woman? I thought he only watched over warriors."

"My heart, *you* are a warrior, don't doubt yourself. My men have adopted you as an informal member of the regiment. They regard it as a high honor to be stationed outside your tent."

"I'm flattered. Even though the Hyksos menace has been removed—"

"For now," Kamin interrupted. "They won't give up so easily. They and their evil god are intent on conquering Egypt. But those concerns are for another day. We can savor the victory for a time."

She nodded. "I feel at ease, being surrounded by your men, soldiers loyal to you."

"By the way, Horus has granted us one further boon—neither will survive the other. Our lives and our deaths are truly linked."

She relaxed into his hold, letting her head fall against his strong shoulder as she had done so many times on their long journey. "Such a fate pleases me like no other could."

"He also told me he would come and serve as a witness for the judging of our hearts, when the time comes."

"May it be many long years away," Nima said. "The Afterlife was beautiful, but I'm in no rush to walk there again."

"Agreed." Kamin nodded. "At least next time we'll go in the proper way, not a back door."

"But still together," she sighed with happiness.

Kamin's eyes were intense. "I refuse to be parted from you again, not in life or death. The Great One promised me."

"Promised *us*," she corrected, drawing him in again for another kiss.

"I have a gift for you, to replace the amulet you lost when we called Renenutet." He got up and crossed to the side table, bringing her a small white leather pouch.

She took it, surprised. "When did you find time to do this?"

"I had to do something while I was cooling my heels in Tentaris. I was a raging lion, penned up there, waiting for Tiy to get his army mobilized. So I commissioned his goldsmith to make this, and I carried it in my belt pouch as my own amulet until the moment I could present it to you, safe and sound and restored to me." He nudged the bag. "Well, open it."

Loosening the thongs holding the tiny sack shut, Nima turned it upside down on the sheets. A golden bangle bracelet fell into her lap. She picked it up, admiring it from all directions. There were miniature golden charms on the bangle—a stylized falcon, a snake, a tiny pair of dancer's finger cymbals, and a tablet bearing miniature hieroglyphics.

Taking the bracelet from her hand, Kamin placed it around her wrist, fingering the tablet charm. "This says, 'Nima, held in Kamin's heart for all time.'"

Suffused with joy and tenderness, Nima rubbed his check softly with her good hand. "My beloved soldier."

She thought he blushed a little under the tan. "You—you like it? We can add a charm when our first son—or daughter—is born. It's not the same as the bead amulet your mother gave you, but—"

Nima turned it on her wrist for a moment, admiring the intricacy of the charms. "Perfect. It's perfect. What can I do for you?" she asked, looking him full in the face and smiling. "You do so much for me—"

"Just love me," he said, gathering her into his arms and lowering his lips to hers.

And so she did, for many long and happy years, until the gods kindly took them both into the Afterlife, together forever as promised.

ABOUT THE AUTHOR

Best-selling, award-winning author Veronica Scott grew up in a house with a library full of books as its heart, and when she ran out of things to read, she started writing her own stories. Married young to her high school sweetheart then widowed, Veronica has two grown daughters, one young grandson and cats. You can usually find Veronica on Twitter, at her blog or on Facebook:

http://veronicascott.wordpress.com/
http://twitter.com/#!/vscotttheauthor
https://www.facebook.com/pages/Veronica-Scott/177217415659637